Metazoan Variations

Evolutionary Fables and Other Emblematic Tales

Mike Bendzela

UnCollected Press

Metazoan Variations

Cover Art: Willie McElroy
Back Matter Photo: Donna Katsiaficas

Book Design by:
UnCollected Press
8320 Main Street, 2nd Floor
Ellicott City, MD 21043

For more books by UnCollected Press:
www.therawartreview.com

First Edition 2020
ISBN: 9781736009888

Foreword

What if Aesop had been a Darwinian?

In the United States "belief" in evolution by natural selection hovers around 19%.[1] The proportion has risen slightly over the years, but that still leaves most Americans stuck in the rut of supernaturalism.

The problem is not lack of information. Many expert writers have produced books and websites over the last century that document exhaustively the achievements of the evolutionary sciences since the publication of *On the Origin of Species* in 1859. Could the beast narrative, too, be fit to teach evolutionary truths?

The problem with using the fable to transmit an evolutionist message is that the form has just about gone extinct. Utterly synonymous with Aesop, the fable comes off now as entirely derivative. Such tales seem too hokey for modern sensibilities, mere children's stories followed by soapbox statements ("morals") that do not suit the sophisticated tastes of an audience steeped in irony, snark, and calculated self-regard.

As the venerable *Treasury of Aesop's Fables* by Oliver Goldsmith tells it:

> Fables are allegorical stories, delivered with an air of fiction, under various personifications, to convey truth to the mind in an agreeable manner. By telling a story of a <u>Lion, Dog,</u> or a <u>Wolf</u>, the Fabulist describes the manners and characters of men, and communicates instruction without seeming to assume the authority of a master or a pedagogue.[2]

Aesop presumably used the fable to disarm those listeners who would be skeptical of wisdom dispensed by a former slave. The form's engaging qualities allowed his subversive messages to be "received with avidity" instead of "scornfully rejected."[3]

His were not just children's concerns. In addition to slavery, Aesop's topics included revenge, jealousy, criminality, deception, greed, suicide, etc., all expressed in narratives that continue to be models of concision. Derived from oral traditions, wherein the pithier the tale, the better the recall (for our probably illiterate fabulist), Aesop's tales perfected the art of narrative economy:

> A viper entering a smith's shop, looked up and down for something to eat, and seeing a File, fell to gnawing it as greedily as could be. The File told him, very gruffly, that he had best be quiet and let him alone; for that he would get very little by nibbling at one, who, upon occasion, could bite iron and steel.

> *Moral: It's the fate of envy to attack those characters that are superior to its malice.*[4]

But Aesop dealt almost exclusively in symbolism, not natural history, a reflection of the era in which he lived, when all believed that the gods had created animals for human uses—from eating to enslavement. That was over 2,500 years ago. Since then, our view of the natural world has been completely transformed.

In his book *The Discovery of Evolution*, Professor of Zoology David Young summarizes the classical view that Aesop shared in:

> Hitherto, the natural world had been regarded largely from a human-centered point of view. It was believed that animals [...] of all kinds had been designed and distributed by God with human needs in mind. Each species was therefore intended to serve some human purpose, which might be practical, moral or symbolic. [...] The chief focus of medieval literature about [...] animals was this rich assortment of moral associations and meanings. The medieval writers garnered these meanings

from old and respected sources. […] They were not concerned to record details of the natural world or to analyze its workings. Hence many a far-fetched tale was handed on because it could be traced back to an authority like Aristotle or one of the later compilers.[5]

Since ancient times, we have revised and updated our view of nature, culminating in the discomposing discoveries of Darwin and his colleague, Alfred Russel Wallace. Even before them, early natural historians "took the crucial step of gradually breaking away from" earlier traditions, such as the Aesopian tradition, "and basing their accounts of animals and plants on their own work. Books on natural history were increasingly compiled from these recent observations, which enabled the writers to set aside many of the old fables as 'errors of the ancients'."[6] It would seem, then, that these story traditions—the fable and its sister species, the parable—beg to be revised and updated as well.

Will such mutated fables and parables be received "avidly" today, rather than "scornfully rejected"? The answer may be in the affirmative, if Darwin's original insight, expressed in *The Descent of Man*, is correct:

...the difference in mind between man and the higher animals, great as it is, certainly is one of degree and not kind.[7]

The truths discovered by Darwin and his descendants are no less fabulous than Aesop's great fictions:

Your father and your mother are great apes.

Your siblings, fellow primates.

Your grandparents, mammals.

Your cousins, placentals.

Your more distant cousins, marsupials and monotremes.

Yet more distant—egg-laying Reptilia and Amphibia!

You hiccup like a frog.

You walk like a fish.

You chew like a shark.

Invasive as the fungi—

Your cells share memories with independent bacterial colonies.

You, then—what, exactly, are you?

Part baboon, part philosopher.[8]

Table of Contents

...if we choose to let conjecture run wild then animals our fellow brethren in pain, disease death & suffering & famine, our slaves in the most laborious work, our companions in our amusements, they may partake, from our origin in one common ancestor, we may all be netted together. (From Charles Darwin's Notebook B.)

PART ONE

Primordial Fables

CHAPTER ONE

The Invertebrates

Ants vs. Termites

Some Formicidae living under a certain wood stump were incapable of realizing they did not know anything of the outside world. Their antennae were exquisitely tuned to find just the airs of their own colony agreeable. The edicts that wafted down from their Queen filled them with an illusion of knowledge and reason. This motivated them to action, which felt to them just like free will.

The Isoptera in a mound nearby had evolved a disposition almost identical to that of the ants: They imagined that the notions radiating from Royal Headquarters issued from their own heads, and they fancied themselves informed about the world.[9]

It was revealed to the ants that the rotten stump under which they nested was the Holy Motherland. But this same stump had been vouchsafed to the termites instead as a delectable corpse.

For the ants, it was an abomination to think of their home being consumed; whereas for the termites it was a sacrilege to waste a corpse! After all, this stump was a gift from On High. They both believed this.

So, when a troop of termites arrived at the stump to consume what was rightfully theirs, the ants were waiting for them—with open jaws that snapped like traps.

The sense of belonging involves elevating group appetite over reason.

Crickets' Doom

Some crickets' (*Gryllus*) eggs hatched, and the nymphs crawled out of the earth, only to find they had become food for toadlets (*Anaxyrus*).

The nymphs succumbed to the toadlets for a while, screeching, "We have met our doom!" But then the nymphs molted their exoskeletons and grew larger and found themselves suddenly able to out-scramble the toadlets.

Yet the toadlets grew as well and caught up with the cricket nymphs and began consuming them in earnest. "We have met our doom!" the cricket nymphs again screeched, but they molted further and soon could scramble ahead of the toadlets.

And on it went, until the crickets matured into adults that hopped on ahead of the toadlets.

But the toadlets eventually became adult toads that hopped after the crickets and gobbled them down. And in this way the crickets finally did meet their doom.

We make much noise of the inevitable.

The Fate of the Samara

A mild and rainy spring made for a fertile season for the red maples (*Acer rubrum*) populating the rocky hillside near a northern lake. One prolific maple especially delighted in the young hanging in festoons from her highest reaches. On a warm breezy day, they spun away from her on papery wings, whirligigs in uncontrolled flight. They all launched outward and downwards—most of them striking the surface of the icy lake to be swallowed by the dark waters.

Others wound up on the sterile rocks to perish in the harsh sunlight. Those that happened to land on the ground were mostly eaten—by insects, worms, birds, and small mammals. Scores became infected with fungi and bacteria and never got to germinate.

Only here and there, years later, did it become clear that a few of these samaras had managed to survive the wastage to become saplings.[10]

Very few—through luck, timing, or good placement—manage to be of consequence in this world.

The Ignominious Ichneumonid

As her pure white pups feed upon their host, Mother Braconid, an ichneumon wasp,[11] attends nearby with pride. It is a nativity scene replicated as through a kaleidoscope—Madonna and Brood— each of her scores of pups a miniature cocoon, diaper-white, attached to an enormous, surrogate wet nurse that functions as a single leaf-green teat.

The caterpillar of the *Manduca* sphinx moth, treated by mother wasp, lies immobilized, now a spectator to its own dissolution. The observer immediately wonders: How does it feel to be eaten alive?

The blissful nursery rhyme is rudely interrupted by Mother *Manduca*: she flaps nearby in her dusty habit, having to witness the immolation of her only hope for a future.

Birth is tenderness compounded with horror.

Locusts

The Acrididae take to the parched field as a cloud, as they are apt to do. The terrified, grain-eating hominins flee in tears and, to appease their gods, cast their infants against a stone shrine to die.

"It doesn't seem right," says one locust to another, "to eat so zealously when it's clear others suffer thus."

Pausing on the stalk it is denuding, the other locust remarks, "Who blames a raindrop for the flood's destruction?"

Low Life

On a rainy afternoon, the hardy banana slug (*Ariolimax*) stretches itself out in daylight, lounging, even. Would that its ancestors could see it now, the marine gastropod-gone-terrestrial, needing no shell for protection. Slime, a shiny substitute for sea water, covers its whole body, lubricating it and making it difficult even for the flat-faced ape to get a good grip on it—to say nothing of the elegant fox, the sneaky raccoon, the flamboyant skunk, the pointy-faced 'possum, the wily pheasant, the obnoxious goose, the crow and the duck, the rattlesnake and the lizard, the frog and the toad. Not one can get a good grip on it. Thus, even the lowly[12] slug makes the predator earn its keep

Parable of the Queen's Colony

As her attendants gather around, issuing praises of a long and fruitful reign, the Queen (*Apis mellifera*) finishes her last round of egg-laying. The queen cups have all been occupied with potential princesses and filled with sacred food and capped over. The top combs are burgeoning with honey. Succession is in the air.

The workers' songs commemorate the thousands lost in defense of the hive when hornet scouts began capturing and decapitating workers at the threshold. As their sisters' bodies and heads lay twitching all around them, valiant warriors surrounded the hornet intruders, clung to them, and scalded the predators to death with their body heat. These are the steadfast gemmules[13] of the old queen that will be passed on to the next generation.

The celebrating city is redolent with wax, honey, and pheromones. These volatile molecules, huge and ornate, catch on the wind and tumble end-over-end for miles.

Nearby, the wet noses of *Ursa americanus* and her cubs begin to twitch from the scent. Trembling with this augury of baby bee flesh, they gallop through the woods and eventually run into a circle of stinging fence wire surrounding the hives.

The mother bear flinches in retreat, but a corner post snaps, allowing her cubs to scramble over to the boxes.

The city topples, the propolis-sealed boxes break open—and a howling whirlwind issues from the hive. The bears feed in this chaos, chewing through combs into the delicious brood larvae that lie ripening in their wax cribs.

The carnage continues—until a rifle crack pierces the air.

A procession of death heralds the successful organism

The Parasite

The thousands of darlings hatched by *Dermacentor albipictus* find their host and settle in. The quarters are cozy, warm, and secure, and the provision plentiful. These ticks each scurry to find a good spot to dig in, and, soon enough, all activity ceases as the feeding begins.

The long interval during which they gorge themselves is like prayer, a period of silence commemorating those billions who have perished: These had clung to underbrush until the bitter end, waiting for a random host that never materialized; then they died of starvation, falling like dust to the forest floor. . . . Now their more fortunate kin swell as, cell by cell, they take in the nourishing blood of their host.

As surely as the sands of time fall to the bottom of the glass, the host animal becomes delirious, wandering out of winter woods and into human habitation, scraping its hide raw against rocks and trees and houses, utterly unaware of what is happening to it.[14]

A little girl parts the curtain in her woodsy home and screams at the ghost moose in her yard—emaciated, fur gone, eyes vacant as empty goblets. By the time the game warden gets there, the moose is dead.

Catastrophe may be enacted in increments.

Snake Eyes

The hawk-moth caterpillar (Sphingidae) was content to hang out on a leaf posing as a snake. It did not realize what it was doing, of course. Neither could it hear the birds shrieking as they fled in fear from the mimic. That is how startlingly authentic the eyes on the larva's snake costume were.[15]

The owl that finally snapped up the caterpillar in its beak was also not aware of what it was doing, and it had to content itself with an appetizer rather than the full meal it thought it had captured.

Deception is ultimately a matter of taste.

Spider Mitts

A jumping spider (*Salticus*) owned a pair of mitts that mesmerized the females.[16] These mitts bristled in such a way as to arouse the appetite and bring all action to a halt. The male would conceal his delectable body behind a leaf and let his mitts—held aloft as advertisements—speak for him: "Juicy Meat!" "Over Here!" The waving of these mitts was done seductively, and the female became rather incapacitated by her hunger. Once she was completely exhausted, the male leaped out to copulate with her, pulling sperm from his pedipalps.

The trick now was to extricate himself before being eaten by his mate.

Advertising oneself deceptively may set the trap, but one had better have good directions for getting out.

11

The Spider's Writing

A field spider (*Argiope*) finished up her web between tall goldenrod plants and hid under a leaf. The orb with its bold zigzag, left to refract the sunlight, caught the attention of a passing vole (*Microtus*), who was immediately struck by the spider's style. Squinting, the vole clearly made out the word MAMMALIAN. What was this spider trying to say? It was undoubtedly something momentous.[17]

The vole rushed off to spread the word that *Argiope* had a message for the small mammals of the field. Soon, a crowd of mammalian spectators pressed in around the vacant web— chipmunk (*Tamias*), squirrel (*Sciurus*), and woodchuck (*Marmota*)— all testing their interpretive skills against the spider's script. They pronounced alongside such long-time rivals as porcupine (*Erethizon*) and raccoon (*Procyon*).

The white-tailed deer (*Odocoileus*) said that it had never witnessed such accord among the beasts of the field. This was short-lived, as multiple interpretations of the oracle arose amongst the various species. The ermine (*Mustela*) even drew blood when it suggested that the message spelled out MUSTILIDAE.

Before carnage could ensue, the spider climbed out onto her web—naturally in a state of distress upon seeing all the animals pressed around—and asked what they wanted.

The vole spoke up: "We have come to read the message you have left us in the center of your web. What does it mean?"

"Nothing," the spider said. She gripped the taut strands of her orb and thrummed it like a drumhead. "It's just a web reinforcement."

The tendency to see design in the random noise of nature is egotism writ large.

Stick Insect

There is a saying among phasmids: "Look dead or be dead."
Leave it to the bats with their motion-detecting sonar to make the lack of visual cues in the phasmids a non-issue.[18]
For this reason, the stick insect excels at doing nothing.

The key to success for some is to be nothing if not nondescript.

Trilobites and the Horn of Wisdom

In an arm of the Ordovician Sea, the trilobites found themselves in crisis: They had dissolved into factions that continually warred over their differences. The megas swam intimidatingly over the micros, who remained rolled up nearly all the time. The spiny ones endlessly harried the smooth ones in molt. The shield-heads sought to exterminate the helmet-heads.[19]

It had gotten so bad that the eldest *Cameroceras*, a tentacled cephalopod, was brought in to settle these disputes.

"The squabbling of you trilobites makes no sense to us," said the Horn of Wisdom, lunging, "for you all taste the same."

Trip to the Skies

While lugging back to the nest the decapitated head of a beetle, a foraging ant of the tribe of carpenters (Camponotini) was struck by a thought so profound it ceased its lugging and stood in awe and wonder.

"I am being called!" the ant realized.

It dropped the beetle head and fell off the chemical trail of its kin to scramble towards the dark forest floor. As it ran, the implications of its calling took root in its mind, and the ant experienced an exhilaration bordering on terror.

It was now clear that, while no queen, this ant would mount to the skies! It just needed to find the proper launch pad from which to fling itself upward.

Delirious with the prospect, the trembling ant stumbled as it mounted the nearest stalk of a forest plant. The outcome was now undeniable: the ant would fly up to the sun and at last comprehend what it was. But first, the ant needed to get a grip on itself: all this scrambling upward was exhausting.

Overheated from excitement, the ant shifted to the cool side of a leaf and hung there in the shade.

"Now calm down!" the ant thought, biting with all its might on a vein of the leaf to anchor its trembling body.

Then, with a chill, it occurred to the ant that this call to flight could all be a dream . . .

In due time, the fruiting body of the *Ophiocordyceps* fungus,[20] its journey through the ant's nervous system now complete, burst out the back of the dead insect's head and extended upward into the darkness, releasing its load of spores.

Those delusions that most impress us with their grandeur propagate freely.

Unwanted Adornments

A fruit fly (*Rhagoletis*) hated some adornments on its tiny, transparent wings. These zigzags, which it was born with, made the fly stand out among its peers.

The other flies were relentless in their put-downs: "Instead of wings, one would think our friend mounted the air on spindly legs!"

At their laughter, a jumping spider (*Salticus*) leaped out of hiding. Sprinting for its prey, the spider stopped short: it mistook the zigzags on the fly's wings for a predator such as itself—another spider!—and turned and fled.[21]

The adorned fly was now given credit for its clever ruse and treated as a hero.

A shameful trait may turn out to be one's best asset.

CHAPTER TWO
Sea Fables

The Ancestral Whale's Fable

A long time ago, in the Tethys Sea, a young *Dorudon* undulated home to report to her mother her close encounter with the predatory *Basilosaurus*. "He said that we were dogs," she wailed, "and that his kind were the True Fish!"

"We are indeed descended from beasts of the field," the mother whale said, "but we are not dogs." She was no slouch when it came to genealogy. "Not that I want you associating with the basilosaurus again, but if you do happen to see him, tell him his ancestors were just as furry-limbed and land-bound as ours were."

"But if we were all land-lumbering beasts," the calf asked, "why are our nostrils so high on our heads?"[22]

"Oh, that's Mother Nature's way of keeping us in touch with the Upper World," the mother answered, by way of wild surmise. "She never wants us to forget where we came from."

Even proper notions of history may become contaminated by belief.

Anglerfish

In the cosmos of the deep, a tiny orb shines. It wavers and glows ember-like, a firefly lost in a starless universe. This glow attracts fish, shrimp, other crustaceans, that become transfixed by the shiny object and simply must go check it out. Is it what they have been longing for, the key to satisfying their appetites, which rage continually in this tight deep?

When they are impelled to take a closer look, the great barbed jaws of the anglerfish (*Ceratias*) snap them up, extinguishing the light from their eyes.

The shiny, false promise, more than any overt threat, lures the unwary to their extinction.

Cuttlefish

A little cuttlefish—one of the seemingly endless iterations of the ancient Mollusca—perceived the presence of the bottlenose dolphin (*Tursiops truncatus*) nearby. Steeling itself, the cuttlefish rippled with color and appeared indomitable.

The dolphin just parted its beak-shaped snout for a bite and said, "You are nothing."

The young mollusk released a quantity of ink in protest: "I'll show you!" The cloud of ink swelled huge; the effect was short-lived, but it fooled the dolphin.

The cuttlefish darted off, its ruse dissipating into a sea that extended dimly in all directions.

Natural selection concerns itself only with the present.

Flounder's Eye

The Atlantic herring (*Clupea*) lived shrewdly in schools and indeed never left them. They wavered above their flatfish neighbor, the flounder (Pleuronectoidei), and informed him of their newest lesson:

"It seems hard to believe, but we are one and the same. Your kind once swam upright like us and had eyes on the right as well as the left side of the head."

Gazing up at these herring, the flounder quipped, "Right and left are myths. The world has two directions—fore and aft—as anyone with eyes can see."

Evolution bestows upon us no native insight into our makeup.[23]

Friend Anemone

Outside of a shell shed by a dead mollusk, the hermit crab (*Dardanus pedunculatus*) appears a pathetic thing, a mere coil of tissue hankering for a home, no matter how modest. The crab takes to the cast-off carapace like a foot to a slipper and drags its sole around, scuffing the sea floor.

As if to amuse itself, the crab uses its claw to prod and pick at small anemones stuck to rocks and other shells, a task for which the hermit crab is well-suited, like a mother adept at prying sticky fingers from stolen candy. Then the crab dons these wriggling, helpless Actiniaria on its shell, like ornate feather hats, till it looks positively absurd.[24]

Incognito scuttles the costumed hermit crab...until a beady-eyed octopus, zeroing in for the kill, pounces on the crustacean and its ornaments, like a lion on a gazelle. Such an easy target! But the cephalopod winces from stings and poison: the anemones' tentacles are armed. It is as if the octopus has tried to engulf a cactus.

Abandoning all hope for a quick meal, the cephalopod gets off its quarry and pulses and flexes out of view, leaving behind, intact, the hermit crab and its showy protectors.

The most modest obtain purpose from unexpected quarters.

Remora, Parasite

The endangered baleen whale (*Eubalaena glacialis*) is an industrious, hard-working animal, having to continually cruise the seas to make a living for herself. She is also renowned for her resentment toward the parasitic *Remoras* that dog her. An increasing number of these species of fish have been seen lately, loitering on whales and dolphins, even on manatees and turtles. The baleen whale, having grown weary of them, turns on them.

"You scavenge our scraps and even our *faeces*," she says. "Why not hide your head in shame?"

"I find it very odd," replies the remora, immediately attaching its sucker head to the underside of the whale's jaw, "that you would think a scavenging, *faeces*-eating creature such as myself would in the least concern myself about what you think of me."

Effacing oneself may effect one's persistence.

Sea Turtle, Run

Seething like baby spiders in their nest, the sea turtles scramble out of their hole.

Onto the beach they race, cameras clicking and whirring nearby at their debut.

The turtles are drawn almost mystically to the watery horizon, several pulling ahead of the pack, flippers working wildly.

Crabs approach awkwardly and kidnap a few.

The frigate bird, the gull, and the vulture dive down to pluck turtles off the beach or right out of the water.

It is all captured on film. Natural selection has never been so photogenic.

Run, turtles!

The numbers of those eaten alive under water by sharks and fish are not recorded.

All the scrutinizing in the world does not satisfy our appetite for inquiry.

The Shark's Blindness

A mother pinniped harbor seal was swimming with its pup back to its favorite rock for a rest, when a tiger shark (*Galeocerdo*) drew a bead on the young one. As the shark launched forward, its nictitating membranes lifted and, like shutters, veiled its eyes from the blood and thrashing flippers.

The mother seal fluttered helplessly around the shark in a cloud of her pup's blood, wailing: "Have you no shame, parting a mother from its child?"

"I saw nothing of the sort," the shark said, disappearing into the deep.

Denial rather protects our self-image as we bull through life.

Tetrapods

A tetrapod follows the tide out in a Late Devonian estuary to seek out a distant relative, the last of the *Acanthostega* line.

Scanning the retreating waters for a while, the tetrapod is at last deeply stirred upon seeing its relative's scaly body undulating out of the water. Its beady eyes stare straight up out of its head, and its limbs look only half-formed.

The tetrapod remarks that the creature looks to be from another world.

"Not so." The creature hauls itself out of the water. "We are much alike. We have a backbone, and a tail that sways as we ambulate. We walk on all fours. Feel my arm—it contains the same bones as yours—"[25]

A commotion from behind interrupts their accord: A troop of tetrapods fans out onto the tidal basin, hissing at the sea creature. They rally around, turning and swatting their tails, driving the beady eyes back beneath the waves.

They admonish the tetrapod, "Have nothing to do with those scum-eaters!"

We dwell on differences at the risk of obscuring our common heritage.

CHAPTER THREE
The Aves and Other Vertebrates

The Allegorical Egg

It is the result of an unbroken lineage stretching back four hundred million centuries to an unknown source, perhaps a little pond[26] somewhere.

No one knows how it got started, but molecule begat molecule, through eras, epochs, even extinctions, arriving on the threshold of yesterday, finally parking *here*, in the nest of this bird (*Turdus migratorius*)—a fragile, blue egg, utterly ignorant of its journey.

Then a wandering black snake (*Pantherophis obsoletus*) slips its insolent head into the nest: sniffing out the egg, the snake opens its jaws to an extraordinary width to fit the whole thing inside its mouth—and away goes the creature that took billions of years to complete but never to hatch, its exquisite and complex history now reduced to feed.

Baby Cuckoo

Unfortunately for the reed warbler (*Acrocephalus*), a mother cannot possibly spend every moment of her life guarding eggs. This mother had gone out only briefly with her spouse for a feeding, when the cuckoo (*Cuculus*) stopped by and deposited one of her eggs—speckled cleverly to resemble the reed warbler's eggs—into the nest.

What is a mother to do? In this case, there was nothing to do but mother. The warbler brooded on the eggs, and the cuckoo hatched first.

It grew fast. Mother and father both continually had to leave the nest behind for spiders, worms, crickets, whatever they could find, to satisfy the monster chick's insatiable stomach.

As the chick grew, it tossed one, then another, and finally all three eggs out of the nest.

The parents continued to stuff the enormous chick's mouth full of arthropods. The chick got so large it broke the nest to pieces.

Finally, fully fledged, it abandoned its parents' care.

The well-adapted parasite kidnaps the affections of others.[27]

The Bowerbird of Papua New Guinea

The bowerbird (*Chlamydera*) spent months building a hut out of sticks that, like he, was not much to look at. It would be the furnishings and decor that would grab female interest. But his eye favored the drab, and how much could one do with a gray pallet?

He spent considerable time gathering fungi from the surrounding forest—brackets, mushrooms, lichens—all in varying shades of drear. Then came the animal turds, hundreds of them, piled in heaps inside his hut. The females were, shall we say, skeptical. He laid out a slate-pebble foyer, adding much lighter snail shells as complement. Bleached bones scavenged from a nearby shoreline provided an effective, if harrowing touch. He carefully arranged it all, with the larger stones and shells standing out front, grading to smaller ones in back, to create the effect of his looming there in his hut with his turds and fungi.[28]

But what really stirred the females was the junk: faded, wooden clothespins; shampoo bottle caps; and a plastic toy dinosaur, all secured from human habitations. And when the bird retired into his hut and imitated a Papuan man *tocking* a wooden post with a mallet, he earned himself a wife.

Love is livelier mediated by art.

The Bronze

A young, domesticated turkey despaired upon learning the truth of his species' pedigree. *Meleagris gallopavo* was not historically sedentary, nor so broad-breasted as to be anchored to the Earth, nor totally reliant on the flat-faced ape to propagate their kind. They used to be agile, wild animals; but no more.

The youngster voiced his anguish to his mother: "We are descended from birds that could fly! We ate nuts, berries, and insects instead of just corn, and we even raised our own families! What happened to us?"

"Success, child," the hen said. "Sometimes you have to cater to the tastes of your benefactor."

The Catbird's Ruse

The brown-headed cowbird (*Molothrus ater*), needing to secret an egg into the nest of a host, left the cow herd in search of a place to lay. She found a lovely home for her egg in a cup nest hidden in a dense growth of escaped rugosa rose bushes near the farm.

When the unsuspecting host, the gray catbird (*Dumetella carolinensis*), returned, it was not fooled by the speckled egg sitting amongst her blue ones and immediately tossed it out of the nest.

The cowbird returned later to check on her egg and was incensed to find it missing. She began ransacking the nest, puncturing blue eggs, and tearing apart the cup-shaped home.[29]

But at the sound of a felid mewing nearby, and suddenly fearing for her life, the cowbird gave up her vandalism and flew back to the safety of the herd.

Sometimes the outrages of the cheater may be undone only by the pranks of the skilled liar.

The Chameleon Leaves

The triumphant Chamaeleonid managed to escape the appalling tedium of her jar and scramble out the kitchen window into an autumnal landscape.

Having thus emancipated herself, the chameleon was now faced with the challenge of what to do next in her new environment. "I will just do as we do in Madagascar," the chameleon reasoned: "take up a position on the nearest branch against a background of leaves and imagine myself green."

However, this chameleon was not in the tropics of Madagascar anymore but the suburbs of New England; and the local feral felid's motion-sensitive eyes, ignorant of such concepts as "green," immediately saw through the chameleon's pretense and tore her legs off.

In matters of survival, place facilitates competence.

Coils

The *Titanoboa*[30] of the Paleocene epoch gazed at the crocodilian with something like adoration. The snake had convinced itself that engaging the croc would be to the benefit of all: Fishes and turtles would be free of a tormentor, the snake would eat well, and the prey itself would gain a purpose in life.

As the boa slung its coils around the crocodile, it whispered reassurances that all would be well hereafter.

"When would that be?" the crocodile inquired. But its brainstem shut down from lack of blood before it could discern the answer.

The instinct for self-acquittal clings to all we do.

The Columbidae

Who knew—once the ground was broken with explosives and shovels; once the drainage tiles and plumbing were laid and the whole works back-filled and inlaid with cobblestone, brick, bronze and marble; once the pumps and light fixtures were installed to bring the fountain of technology to life—that the most sophisticated modern sculpture garden ever built would be taken over by pigeons?

They strut the stones and stairs, and coast on soft wings through archways, and foul the entire site with droppings, as they have been doing for millennia[31] —from Delphi, to the Valley of the Kings, to Shuruppak.

Constancy is an illusion of abbreviated time.

Copycats

The irrepressible whippoorwill (*Caprimulgus vociferus*) spent its evenings practicing its song, *ad infinitum.* It was the species' universal theme, but there was no sense or moral to it, least of all to those outside the species forced to listen.

Whippoorwill-whippoorwill-whippoorwill sprung like a rumor from every quarter, until soon local mockingbirds were chanting the tune. Even catbirds became contaminated with the call;[32] but in their beaks, this was nonsense, even an outright lie.

When the ground-dwelling apes had finally had enough of it, they slammed their windows shut and drew the curtains.

But, as if to propagandize on behalf of their noisy cousins, cockatiels in their cages sang covers of the tune to their ape captors, over and over, like gospel.

That which persists, prevails.

Creeper

In a stand of dead elms, while sap suckers (*Sphyrapicus*) put up a racket and nuthatches (*Sitta*) launched to and fro, a chunk of bark seemed to come loose on one tree and move sideways across the trunk.

This young brown creeper (*Certhia americana*) lamented to his father that they did not have the colorful adornments of the other birds. "Will we ever look like them?"

"Not in a million years."

The young one marveled at the gaudy clamor of the pileated woodpecker (*Dryocopus*).

"We're so drab and quiet."

"Not another *peep* out of you."

The young creeper crouched on a limb and watched the woodpecker drum and yammer on a dead elm branch. A red-tailed hawk (*Buteo jamaicensis*) swooped in and snatched the noisy woodpecker right off the limb.

The creeper looked at his father. His father said nothing.

The struggle for fitness inspires anonymity as much as notoriety.

Dart Frog

Through ages of bitter experience, the toucan (*Ramphastos*) had learned not to touch the gaudy dart frog (*Ranitomeya*) as its skin was highly poisonous. In a brilliant stroke, the ancestors of this frog had developed a distinctive color pattern, an advertisement of toxicity, that warned the toucan to keep back.

When it became clear how well this dual strategy worked to protect the dart frog, there inevitably arose plagiarists. Several of the frog's less-toxic cousins developed cheap knockoffs of the brightly colored design to share in the protection from the predations of the toucan.[33]

The dart frog remained insouciant. It saw that the toucan had simply picked off those that did not resemble him.

But the spider monkey (*Ateles*) jeered at these other frogs and their transparent mimicry: "Your color compares to the dart frog's the way tree bark compares to tasty fruit."

"So what?" the mimics said. "The toucan never touches us."

A Flash of Wing

The mockingbird (*Mimus*) is adept at defending her territory, even berry-laden bushes, and especially her nest.

She wastes no time winging out and dive-bombing after a predator that approaches her nest of eggs, no matter how large, and will recognize her foe for life.

But in this instance, the intruder happens to be rush-hour traffic, which is about the worst thing that can happen to a mockingbird's neck.

It is horrifying to witness someone clinging to notions that have lost their usefulness.

From Froglet to True Frog

Their metamorphosis now complete, the froglets (*Rana*) migrated out of the pond *en masse* and immediately set about gobbling down every Caelifera grasshopper nymph they could see. But as these baby grasshoppers emerged from the earth they molted and began to grow and hopped out of the froglets' reach. "Whatever shall we do?" shrilled the froglets, "the grasshopper nymphs have outstripped us!"

"Hop harder!" their mothers cried.

As these froglets matured they were able to galumph forward with more *elan* and gobble down the grasshopper nymphs again. But the grasshopper nymphs kept molting: they shed their exoskeletons and grew larger bodies, which allowed them to outstrip the froglets.

"The grasshopper nymphs have escaped us again!" shrilled the froglets.

Their mothers just repeated, "Hop harder!"

And on it went, the froglets growing and galumphing forward, gobbling up nymphs, which molted and outstripped the froglets ... until one day some mature frogs caught up with adult grasshoppers—which up and flew away! And in this way the frogs learned Darwin's great lesson: The better you become, the more incompetent you be.[34]

Heron Bait

"Remember—your appetites benefit the health of this pond," the matron *Lithobates clamitans* tells her brood of growing tadpoles. "Keep nibbling at the green algae else it multiply out of control and starve the pond of life!"

Indeed, as the tadpoles check the algae with their feeding, the pond hosts multitudes. But why should the beneficent tadpoles then disappear without a trace, and so suddenly?

The great blue heron (*Ardea herodias*) swoops down and poises in knee-deep waters, standing as still as the cattails that tower near him. The pond's tranquil aspect has his complete attention, and his neck coils almost imperceptibly, like a vine tracking sunlight.

One stick-like leg lifts without making a ripple as he steps forward—then that neck discharges a sharp bill beneath the water's surface.

The heron swallows its prey whole.

Little kindnesses are but morsels in the struggle for dominance.

Horned Lizard

An indomitable ant (*Pogonomyrmex*) is held in high esteem in the desert for its civilized teamwork. The nest harbors a populace fiercely loyal to the Regent, a superb and complex system of communications experts, and an army equipped with the deadliest weapons known to the whole world of Hymenopterans.

Foragers find seeds in the most unlikely places and haul them back to the great mound. There, workers grind up the seeds and put away large stores of bread in granaries, singing praises to their brave patrollers.

The foragers also bring news back to the nest: If a rodent alien has been spotted nearby interfering with the foragers' work, an army is drummed up. They swarm the enemy by the hundreds and sting it repeatedly until it is dead. Then they return in triumph to the mound, breaking bread with the Queen.

But one day the steady stream of seed foragers filing back to the mound suddenly tapers off. The news is disturbing: an alien is not just interfering with the foragers but exterminating them.

The army issues forth from the mound, stingers bristling. They find the intruder—a horned lizard (*Phrynosoma*)—snapping up foragers in its mouth and swallowing them whole. The army overwhelms the beast, stinging it over every inch of its squat spiny body.

The lizard sits as unfazed as a statue.

The most formidable adaptations are no guarantee against the contingencies of nature.

How Archaeopteryx Learned to Fly

Archaeopteryx engaged a rival in feathered combat for the benefit of the females that had gathered to watch. In this arch display of the Jurassic Period, long, ornate tails swished like bridal trains, and clawed forelimbs held aloft dark capes of finery.

As the females hissed and tightened their circle around the rival, it became clear that our *Archaeopteryx* was outmatched: the other's ornamentation, with its iridescent splendor, had caught their eye more.

In desperation, our suitor leaped onto the bole of a fallen cycad tree, scrambled to the high end above the fray, held out his cape for all to see—and jumped!

His regalia now buoying him up like a spirit, *Archaeopteryx*[35] sailed out beyond his rival, drawing along a parade of shrieking females after him.

Sex makes geniuses of the most unlikely candidates.

The Leap

The petite mother theropod hovered over a circle of little eggs, as her brood of baby reptiles broke their shells and uncurled in the sunlight. The hatchlings immediately stretched, wriggled, and flicked their tongues, hissing for their first insect meal. They all had long bodies like their mother, and yellow stripes like their father.

With one egg yet to go, the mother scrambled to keep her babies fed. Then something astonishing happened: The remaining egg developed a sudden breach; a conical object came into view. Gradually, the rest of the head emerged, clothed entirely in fine down, its snout compressed down to a single, horny stub.[36]

Curious, the mother and her brood watched as the creature freed itself from the shell. Its body was plump, not long; and hirsute, not smooth and striped. Even its forelimbs were clothed in down. And instead of hissing, it emitted a series of notes that alarmed the young reptiles.

The mother did not like what she saw; so she turned and with one snap of her jaws broke the mutant's neck.

Natural harmony necessitates a general continuity.

The Lowly Molothrus

To the delight of her friends, the phoebe (*Sayornis*) shouted from a limb: "Look at the pathetic cowbird! She is like a fly herself, traipsing along amongst piles of cow shit."

The cowbird responded simply, "We all have our ways, Miss Phoebe."

But the cowbird's companion said, "Why meet such abuse with kindness? I'd show her a thing or two—"

The cowbird checked her friend with: "Little does she know, I just laid my egg in her nest."

Deception maintains a placid bearing, causing us to mistake opportunists as simpletons.

The Mockingbird's Acolyte

A particular female *Mimus* sits rapt in the leaves as a male new to these parts perches upon the highest stick against bottomless blue and lets fly. He cobbles together for his listener a hoax consisting of clichés and flapdoodle drawn from his competitors.

When an irritated *Cardinalis* stops by to investigate who is impinging on his airwaves, he immediately recognizes the fraud and flaps off, disgusted. Then a male bluebird (*Sialia*) swoops in to ward off the plagiarist, but the mockingbird stands his ground and drives the bluebird away.

The female shifts her footing on her perch, and the male resumes his sermon. The titmouse (*Baeolophus*) and the towhee (*Pipilo*) are not buying it. But a red-tailed hawk (*Buteo*) is drawn in; and when it perches nearby, intrigued, the mockingbird leaps from his perch spewing curses and hisses, until the big predator leaves the scene.

At this point, the female moves in to request a nest mate.

The persistent sectarian finds an audience.

Monitor Lizards vs. Cobras

Some monitor lizards (*Varanus*) opposed to the increasing presence of cobras (*Ophiophagus*) in their midst held a public meeting to air their concerns.

One outspoken lizard said to those gathered, "Fellow Lizards! The cobras intend to surround us, defeat us, and take our land. But they won't stop there; we all know how snakes are. If we don't do something quickly, they will swallow all our young!"

Inflamed by this speech, the lizards quickly mobilized. They sought out the snakes, surrounded them, and defeated them. But for reasons no one has been able to fathom, the triumphant lizards then devoured every snake egg they could find.

The most depraved acts may be committed in the name of preventing depravity.

Mother Geese

The fox (*Vulpes*) was quick to point out an unnatural pairing of two Canada geese (*Branta*) who had built a nest on a beaver lodge.

For their part, the beavers (*Castor*) saw nothing amiss: male and female geese look identical to one another, as is true of beavers and foxes as well, and these two seemed content to take turns guarding the nest of eggs and foraging at the water's edge.[37] Even though the geese were occupying the lodge, they did nothing to disturb the beavers' way of life.

"But they're both females," the fox moralized. "Can you imagine the filth that transpires between them?"

"No, we can't," a beaver answered. "Our imaginations are not as befouled as yours is."

The Murmuration

The invader starlings (*Sturnus*) make themselves at home with abandon: Innumerable birds adorn every branch and limb of an enormous, denuded maple tree. They are deep in conversation, a chattering mass.

Then something remarkable happens: they all shut up at once and take flight. It is like the bursting of a silent fireworks shell. A coal-black chrysanthemum swells, its spherical shape pulled to a point as birds are drawn off to flee to who-knows-where.

But no: They swing right back around, capriciously, like a comic book illustration of a bee swarm, pour back onto the branches of the tree, and resume their chatter.

Conformity broadcasts its truth: individuals are of little note.

Out on a Limb

Some time ago, there was a species of pigeon (*Ectopistes migratorius*)[38] that shadowed the success of the flat-faced ape whose descendants had become farmers. These pigeons simply took to the country that the farmers had cleared of predators, and they scoured the vast stretches of land, unimpeded.

Thus, they thrived almost despite themselves. Their numbers swelled to such astonishing proportions that some of the more cautious pigeons began to question the wisdom of allowing vast hordes to rifle through the landscape.

Once, they had all gathered on the branches of the pines in some great woods, when the trees began to groan under the weight of all the birds. The doubting pigeons then chirped up:

"We have grown well beyond a supportable capacity!"

"Nonsense!" replied an elder. "One egg per brood hardly constitutes a prolific species—"

Before the elder could finish speaking, a large limb broke, spilling mothers, fathers, and chicks into a heap on the ground below.

Anticipating the nay-sayers, the elder said, "That limb was obviously too weak to support any number of birds and would have broken anyhow."

Sound judgment seldom keeps pace with good fortune.

Parrots

A typhoon stranded some budgies (*Melopsittacus*) on an island occupied by mynah birds (*Gracula*). After acclimating to the new place, the vagrant budgies decided to settle in as best they could. They realized they would have to coexist with the mynahs, but who would rule?

At the budgies' insistence, a troubling philosophical difference first needed to be resolved:

Traditionally, the mynahs had always held that the ovum existed posterior to the hen, and consensus about this had been maintained seemingly forever.

"Who has ever seen an ovum but that comes from the hen?" the mynahs asserted.

But the budgies instead believed that the ovum preceded the hen, and amongst them, too, the uniformity of opinion was quite strong.

"No hen has ever arrived but by ovum," the budgies countered.

So, the budgies passed a resolution declaring the egg supreme and disseminated it to the mynahs to contemplate.

The mynahs accused the budgies of merely parroting an ideology, and they thoroughly rejected the budgies' proposal.

The budgies, incensed as a body, charged the mynahs with putting party politics ahead of scientific truth and with stalling accord on the issue. Speech after budgie speech reiterated this charge.

The mynahs burst into spontaneous chants of protest; and disgusted with the budgies' transparent propaganda, they fell on their necks and drove them from the island.

In politics, confirmation of the facts is beside the point.

The Passerby

A red-tailed hawk (*Buteo jamaicensis*), having finished a feast of marmot, contents itself by settling high in a blue spruce tree to watch the land moving with life below.

Some corvids roosting nearby are having none of it, though, and, shrieking, sail directly at the bird of prey, diving at it menacingly, even pelting it with their own bodies.

The hawk swoops off and launches upward, the incensed corvids in black pursuit, wailing, scrambling madly in protest, until—a thousand feet up—the hawk simply pulls in its wings and falls away from its tormenters.

It is adaptive to avoid becoming embroiled in parochial matters.

Preening

The great albatross (*Diomedea*) preened herself in front of a penguin (*Spheniscus*) that bobbed in cold waters near the rock on which the great bird stood.

"She must feel pretty silly," the albatross inferred upon seeing the penguin's pitiful fin stumps. "Is she fish or beast? I don't think even she knows." The great bird continued straightening her magnificent feathers.

Just then the penguin launched out of the water and with addled gait took up a stance on the rock not far from the other bird, and she began preening in like manner.

As the penguin drove her beak into the stubby feathers of her breast, and picked around under her forelimb, and shook her head rapidly back and forth, the albatross recognized, with horror, that those miserable fin stumps were wings just like her own; and, cantilevering her capacious wings over the edge of the rock, the scandalized bird took her preening elsewhere.

Homology is the final humiliation for those who believe they are above nature's dross.

The Smiling Toads of Darwin's Bluff

An obscure species of *Bufo* inhabits a remote point of land called Darwin's Bluff. Long ago, one of these toads learned to smile, but this was a fluke: It was born with a congenital defect of the jaw.

Like most toads, it spent its days in an inconspicuous spot in the dirt, just sitting. There it smiled.

Some crickets fresh from molting had been schooled in the appearance of various predators of the bluff—a disturbingly long course of study for these nymphs. Upon emerging from the earth these crickets fed cautiously. But a few of the more amiable insects were attracted to the new smiling thing in the dirt.

The same went for some grasshoppers, slugs, flies, and beetles.

Even some spiders and small mice were attracted to the smile in the dirt.

And now all the toads of Darwin's Bluff are smiling.[39]

Trade

Poor mother carrion crow (*Corvus corone*), burdened with one egg too many—and not even her own at that. A great spotted cuckoo (*Clamator glandarius*) has put one over on the enterprising corvid—and now a giant interloper threatens to outcompete all the other chicks in the nest. All seems hopeless—right up until the moment a feral neighborhood felid sets her eye on the chicks.

Mother crow sees the cat and puts up a raucous fuss.

At the merest stir of trouble, the parasitic baby cuckoo instinctively farts, as is her wont.[40] The other chicks and their mother reel from the stench. What next?

The smell is too much for the felid as well, and she flees. There is more fragrant prey to be had elsewhere.

Mother corvid bids the stinking interloper a grim, resigned welcome.

The relations we inherit become noxious necessities.

The Turkey's Dilemma

Continually cocking an eye skyward, the turkey hen (*Meleagris gallopavo*) admonished her chicks: "When you see black vying against the blue, run and hide!"

Most chicks obeyed, cowering under the sweet fern, but one inquisitive jake could not help eying a crow (*Corvus*) that had landed in the meadow.

"I am not a hawk, nor an owl," the crow informed the jake.

"Then let's forage together."

"Of course!"

As the jake and crow studied the ground as a pair, the hen ran out and chased the crow away.[41] She then dealt with her incautious child in a most pitiless manner.

True freedom from depredation may mean confinement to the familiar.

Waxwings

In the orchard during bloom season, two waxwings (*Bombycilla cedrorum*) perch at the top of a Yellow Transparent apple tree (*Malus domestica*) in full regalia. She and he wear the same black mask: they are a pair.

He has a white apple blossom petal in his bill. He hops over to the female, holds out the petal and seems to say, "Here, accept this token of my love."

She takes the petal in her bill and hops off in the opposite direction. She stops as if thinking better of it, then hops back over and returns the petal to him, as if saying, "I'd better not."

He takes the petal in his bill and hops down the limb, crestfallen. He stops, then hops back over to her.

She takes the white petal in her bill and hops away with it.

They swap the petal back and forth like this, for several minutes, until she swallows it, and they fly off together.

The charm of ritual lies in its pointlessness.

PART TWO

Prehistoric and Historical Fables and Parables

CHAPTER FOUR

The Mammals

The Insectivores

Beneath the tails and claws of great saurians that tore into one another during the Cretaceous Period, the Earth teemed with little insectivores.[42] These mammals congregated densely around the dung fields of the saurians, for the fields were rife with the arthropods the insectivores lived on.

While mostly nocturnal, working under the cover of night, these creatures still needed a certain amount of guts to make the dash into the open to chase after a winged meal. They knew not to spend too much time foraging for beetles among the turds, as many a mighty saurian foraged on the insectivores themselves as toothsome additions to their diets.

Dams instinctively kept close by their pups; but in a frenzy, it was not unheard of for a parent to flee a pup impaled on the claws of a dinosaur. Those that made it to adulthood preferred to hunt in gangs, but it was always with the full knowledge that one's insectivore comrades might turn tail and run.

To persist among tyrants, one must have a stomach for nausea and shame.

The Late Dinohippus

The horse (*Equus*) and its cousin *Dinohippus*[43] fed together in a handsome woods-lined margin along the rolling plains during the Pliocene Epoch.

As they grazed on the fresh, spring grasses between dwindling piles of snow, a branch dropped from a tree. The horse bolted, shrieking, "Rattlesnake!"[44]

Dinohippus looked up in amusement and disgust. "You can come down off that hill now. It's just a stick."

The horse rejoined its mate to continue grazing; but almost immediately a large tree began swaying. "Giant bird!" The horse was off again in a cloud of dust. It looked back over its shoulder to see its cousin grinning.

"That was just the wind."

When the horse returned, *Dinohippus* moralized to its cousin: "It's possible to stay on our toes without running off in a panic."

At that moment, a shrub began to rustle, and the saber-tooth (*Smilodon*) tackled *Dinohippus* to the ground.[45] The last thing it saw was its cousin's hooves flying in a cloud of dust.

Irrational panic remains as perennial as the spring.

Fishy Heritage

The fennec fox (*Vulpes zerda*) and the Egyptian mongoose (*Herpestes ichneumon*) did not necessarily get along together and in fact rarely crossed paths in the desert. But they did share a distinct pride in their common history.

In these mammals' arid, dryland habitat lay the remains of whales, all extinct, their ocean environs having long-since dried up.[46] The fox and the mongoose stepped around the bones of these creatures, even cordoned them off, to preserve them from damage.

They railed at the very elements for wearing the fossils away, and dutifully brushed aside the shifting sands, as if time itself were the enemy of local tradition. These bones had to be protected and commemorated, for they were the source of their most sacred fibs.

"We must not forget how our ancestors struggled against these predatory fish," the fox said. "Their incursion from the sea nearly wiped us out. Here they shall remain, as reminders of our superior status."

"A grandfather on my mother's father's side fought in the war of independence from these fishes," the mongoose added.

Our ignorance rarely prevents us from celebrating the impossible.

The Termite Nest

The great anteater (*Myrmecophaga*) enjoys humping her baby over to the food hole to show her how properly to eat. The little one observes curiously from the mother's hairy back while she pulls open the earth with her claws to release the delectable food that these creatures delight in.

This substance is as animated as water, flowing out of the earth of its own accord. Mother inserts the funnel of her snout into the well and begins slurping in the rising flood.[47]

Baby gets hungry just watching and wants to try it out herself. But she pauses, hearing a noise, something distant and plaintive, the whine of hordes in distress.

"Mama," she asks, "what is that sound?"

"That's just the food flowing," the mother says. "And the louder the sound, the sweeter the feed!"

The moral horizon extends only as far as is sensible.

The Rodents of Oak Island

The squirrels (*Sciurus*) of Oak Island lived in stick-constructed drays high in the tops of the oak trees and yapped and squalled like frogs or monkeys. The chipmunks (*Tamias*) lived in underground tunnels and chipped and chirped like frogs or birds.

The squirrels spent hours hauling acorns to thousands of caches strewn throughout the island, while the chipmunks spent just as much time stockpiling stores in their underground burrows. The acorns of Oak Island were a delicacy to them all and so plentiful that the populations of both species bloomed to capacity.

They lived side-by-side peacefully, stocking their respective larders, until the year the rains stopped, and a strange conjunction of borers, caterpillars and fungi brought the oaks low. The supply of acorns went into steep decline, and the squirrels and chipmunks found themselves at loggerheads over food.

The squirrels' method of storage began to outrage the chipmunks: the squirrels inevitably forgot where many of their caches were, and the precious nuts would go to waste.

The chipmunks started noticing where the squirrels were burying their acorns, and when the squirrels were not looking, they dug up the caches of acorns and stole away to their cellars with them.

But the squirrels got wise to this, and whenever a chipmunk was around, they would pretend to bury their acorns in a certain spot while really secreting them into their cheeks, then taking them elsewhere to be buried.

Unbelievable as it may seem, there came a time when every acorn on the island was spoken for. All nuts had either been stuffed into chipmunks' cheeks and taken underground or secreted away by the squirrels into innumerable little caches. There was nothing left to do but retire for the winter and see what happened, the chipmunks in their tunnels, the squirrels in their tree nests. And when the food ran out, squirrel and chipmunk alike began to starve.

The more similar the type, the more acute the competition.[48]

As Numerous as the Hares

The hares (*Lepus americanus*) enjoyed a reproductive frenzy but then ran into problems: it seemed they had outstripped the land that once sustained them. When it was suggested that perhaps they were too fruitful, the cry was, "No! The lynx and coyote that check us have fallen in numbers, and that's a good thing!"

When it was observed that the best copses were being occupied at an alarming rate, the response was, "This is the result of encroachment on our habitat by other species!"

When the shocking news arrived that half of the browsing materials had been denuded, officials declared the problem not to be the number of mouths but the relative inaccessibility of the other half.

When a scrawny buck lost half his children to starvation, the others said, "You're a scoundrel who doesn't know how to provide for his own family!"

"We have been reduced to chasing after mice!" the buck cried. "If we don't do something, we could all starve!"

This aroused needless panic. Hares rifled through the undergrowth and hoarded what they could, just in case.

After thousands had died, the scrawny buck was attacked and killed for inciting a riot.

Moralizing about population is fruitless.

Obligate Carnivores

When the hares went into their scheduled population decline, the rugged *Lynx canadensis* was thrown off its usual dietary haunts and began to scour the margins of the adjacent farmland for voles, mice, rats, any other small mammals that wouldn't put up too much of a fight.

It hunkered down and eyed a smallish marmot digging out the entrance to a burrow under a stone wall.

Little did the lynx know that another entity had its keen eye on the marmot. When it sprang forward to grab the rodent, the lynx ran headlong into the red-tailed hawk (*Buteo jamaicensis*), which had swept in from far beyond the lynx's ken and—snagging the marmot in curved talons—managed to avoid a tussle with the lynx and flap off with the prey.

Species seemingly worlds apart find their intersection in common appetites.

Woodchuck's Warning Cry

The marmot said, "There is a terrible fate hanging over us. I have the marks in my flesh that prove it." This woodchuck showed all who cared to look the parallel seams scoring his furred flanks, now beginning to heal over. "I was dropped at the last minute."

The other marmots simply chewed their greens and stared into the field.

"It is this open feeding that exposes us!" the chuck said. "We are safe only in our cellars."

The chucks paused in their feeding and cocked an eye upward. Seeing nothing, they said, "We don't believe you."

The marmot hustled into the middle of the field, stood up, and scanned the horizon. He waited until the bird showed up, then looked back over his shoulder to see if the clan saw. When the red-tailed *Buteo* snatched the woodchuck off the ground, his shriek seemed to split the sky in two.

The impotent long for vindication to their own detriment.

Ovis

Sheep wheel across the green cropped hill like pigeons in flight, several specks of coyote in pursuit.

The sheep suddenly switch back—again like a flock of birds banking—stampeding when there is no place to stampede to.

The mob splits in half—half fleeing uphill, the other down—and when one straggler lamb falls behind, the coyotes pounce. A plaintive whine erupts and then is silenced.

The other sheep remain untouched, freely relinquishing a particle to spare the mass.

They stream and clump at the far end of the field, like flotsam after a storm, the clump loosening a little in relief, then standing immobilized.

The one lamb has finally gained its independence—and a separate identity—in death. But the others are not acknowledging it: they are still fixated on those canids.

The safety of numbers is a product of terror.

Coy Wolf

"Why do you dogs hate us so?" the sheep asked the canid. It was a rare encounter, the sheep bunched up against the banks of a brook, the coy wolf, off the beaten path and having just eaten, amused to find potential prey speaking to him.

"It's not hatred so much as contempt for your uniformity. Even now, I can't tell which of you just dared speak to me."

The demotion of distinction makes murder palatable.

Ruminants

A clutch of ruminants, all horns and hide, flee the big carnivore. The genus does not matter; it is a template followed across the continents. The ruminants clump and scatter, bolt and zigzag, the carnivore chugging along behind, rippling like a seal in a fast current, paws barely treading ground. The ruminants rumble like distant thunder, a stampede engendered by the carnivore's jaws. They churn up a cloud of dust that makes navigation impossible and streak blindly across the plains. It is a spectacle staged on behalf of their own necks.

With fear as driver, the campaign runs itself.

Lone Canid

A coyote pup not keen on play fighting recoils from the bites of her brothers. They run into her and attempt to wrestle her to the ground. She goes off and sulks by herself. It is just her way.

Almost as an afterthought, she wanders away from the den one day and never returns. There will be no more group hunting for her. She pounces on mice, rats, voles, chases down chipmunks, gulps down frogs and berries.

She has learned to be inconspicuous, to avoid the larger wolves and bobcats. While other dogs hunt in packs, she watches them from the shadows.

One day a pack strands a fawn in a field, preparing for a kill. She recognizes her family and springs forward to assist; but they rebuff her with growls and raised fur. Her brother runs into her in an attempt to knock her down. This is not play: he is telling her she is not welcome back. Maybe they do not recognize her anymore.

She will live fully outside the pack now, and nothing can readmit her.

One bears the costs of isolation to maintain a distinct identity.

The Shapeshifter

One cool evening, the feral felid starts at a sudden skitter in the leaves; and she is spurred most helplessly into a leap, shifting unconsciously to her pounce mode, the one she uses on voles, rats, mice, any small skittering mammal like this creature; but what she takes to be a rodent suddenly launches vertically and bursts into musical flight—a woodcock (*Scolopax*), it turns out—much to the cat's surprise.

To thrive, affect to be one thing; be another.

Rats, etc.

Rats, mice, and voles (Myomorpha) tend toward monoculture.[49] Pups fall out of their mothers' fur like dust and wriggle to life. This translates into enough mice, voles and rats to feed the feral felid, the rugged lynx, the lone canid, the vicious stoat, the flamboyant skunk, the barn owl, the red-tailed hawk, the rattlesnake, the elegant fox, the sneaky raccoon, and feed them all nonstop.

These pups vanish as soon as they are birthed, it seems. But their mothers go on birthing more voles, rats, mice, doomed to the consciousness that they are dropping their children into an insatiable maw.

Ages of selection for rampant proliferation ensue, but no monoculture materializes.

The rat, the vole, and the mouse still dream of rippling plains of soft furred flesh, horizons stocked with baby rodents—not a predator in sight.

The deepest instincts that motivate us may remain unfulfilled.

Food Chain

Once their tunnels had become stocked with earthworms, the moles (*Scalopus aquaticus*) could rest and contemplate their good fortune.

"The world is obviously designed with our interests in mind," they said, "as this stock of worms testifies."

Their contentment was disrupted when black rat snakes (*Pantherophis obsoletus*) discovered the moles' tunnels. The snakes feasted on the moles, multiplied, and spread to other tunnels. Thus, the mole's quaint view of the world was extinguished.

"The world is here for our taking," the snakes concluded. "We've been blessed with this cornucopia."

As the snakes increased, they caught the eye of red-tailed hawks (*Buteo jamaicensis*) perched high in the trees. The snakes began to suffer from raptor attacks, even as the moles went into decline from their feeding. The snakes' reign was ended.

"Who else sees the world as completely as we do?" the hawks observed. "We have been so positioned to take advantage of all that we can behold."

The hawks' preeminence was short-lived: hominins and their arrows made sure of that.

Conceit is a natural state of mind.

Afternoon of the Fawns

The white-tailed doe (*Odocoileus virginianus*) sailed over the hood of the car but did not quite clear it: the windshield caught her hoof and sent her end-over-end and crashing to the pavement. But she got back up on her hooves and clattered off into the woods—her twin fawns trotting along behind her.

She told them she just needed to lie down for a minute. Then she would be fine.

Her fawns waited while she rested on the grass. They fed on shrubbery and buds nearby in the meantime and did not stray far from their mother's resting place.

After several days, the twins began to argue: What should they do about mother?

"We should try and wake her."

"No, we need to be patient and let her rest."

They stood and stared, unsure what to do, until they saw that she had begun moving.

They both agreed it was time for her to get up and go; but upon inspecting their mother more closely—putting their noses down there to let her know they were nearby—they were shocked by the stench and found that the movement indicated her hide had become a sack full of maggots.

An awareness of the ubiquity of mortality marks the onset of the mature view of life.

The Carcass

The lone canid came upon the remains of a doe, whose denuded ribcage still had some flesh on it. It was not the meal the coyote wanted, but a long drought had swept the landscape clean of easy prey.

The sudden disturbance of thousands of flies nearly caused her to turn away from the corpse—when the hunkered shapes of several buzzards (*Cathartes aura*) touched down nearby. They sneered and hissed for the canid to clear out.

The canid took up a defensive posture and, surprising even herself, snapped and growled with such ferocity that the carrion birds abandoned all hope and fled the scene.

Competition makes the meager precious.

The Naive Voles

The life of the vole (*Microtus*) is restricted to the orchard, where they feed on plants and roots, and tunnel incessantly. They strive to stay below ground as much as possible, for the open air horrifies them: and the sun is deplorable! But no matter how careful they are to stay among the roots and stones, the barn owl (*Tyto alba*) continually picks them off. It does so without enmity.

Each new loss shakes the population of voles: Where have the missing ones gone? What does the owl do with them? The owl strikes like lightning and leaves no clues. Is she treating them well? Perhaps they should ask.

One day as the owl sits in an apple tree, the voles migrate out of the sod and appear before the owl. The owl turns her head in wonder as the voles amass around the base of the apple tree.

A vole speaks: "What have you done with our comrades? May we have them back?"

The owl nods vigorously—is she trying to say something?—and at that moment releases an object that falls to the ground.

The voles surge forward for a look: There on the grass lies a round, vole-sized pellet of fur and hair, encapsulating a jumble of tiny vole bones.

Nothing prepares the untutored for the news of the world.

The Curious Sciurid

One sultry summer evening, a little brown bat (*Myotis lucifugus*) slips early from her sleep under the barn roof shingles and drops into the crepuscular air.

While swooping after moths, she spies, at the woods line, a commotion—two creatures in flight.

When she wheels around to investigate, she can scarcely believe her tiny eyes: a sort of over-sized, bat-like creature grabs onto the trunk of a tall pine tree and clings there, wings folded under its furred limbs, while an owl banks and turns to make a second pass at it.

The bat flits back toward the barn—by now her relatives are streaming into the failing light—and she chirps out: "You have to get a load of this."

The others follow her over to the woods just in time to view a curious spectacle: an owl swooping down for a snatch, while at the bottom of the tree a sneaky raccoon climbs upward—in the middle, the winged mammal clings to the trunk.

The bats flit around, incredulous: "Impossible!"

"That thing will never be able to take wing!"

Just then this "thing"—a flying squirrel (*Glaucomys sabrinus*)—leaps away from its pursuers, plummets toward the ground on hilariously inept wings,[50] and glides quietly into the forest gloom.

Perfection is no prerequisite for utility.

Boreal Counselor

"Owl, might you reflect on my plight?"

The owl swivels her head around 180 degrees, shocked to find the winged sciurid high in the pine tree, at the edge of her nest. She turns her full, disk-shaped face toward the animal and bores into it with black eyes.

"Please hear out the lowly sciurid."

The owl is so dumbfounded she can say nothing.

The flying squirrel continues. "I am a beast that other beasts mock or pursue to death, one who takes wing with birds who shun him or hunt him down. There is no creature in the forest that does not look askance upon me. Why am I not fit for this world?"

The stumped owl can do nothing but hiss. The squirrel startles, leaps into the air and glides to the safety of the next tree over, convinced that the owl is right.[51]

To Be a Bat

The curious sciurid wished to be admitted to the order Chiroptera, "for the Aves just laugh at me," he said. This flying squirrel had staged several demonstrations for the many orders of birds; but the songbirds and the woodpeckers mobbed him and chased him off, while the falcons and owls tried to seize him. The sciurid got away each time.

The bats could see his point. The sciurid was as furry, warm-blooded, and winged as they were. Sciurids shared some of the bats' dietary habits, fed at night, and nursed their young. But the bats were still left scratching their heads. So, they offered the sciurid a trial membership to see how he would fare as a Chiropteran.

It was soon apparent the flying squirrel could not perform as well as the bats. They could stay aloft for hours, and they cleverly located their prey through sound rather than sight. The flying squirrel could do none of this. But the sciurid did discover how properly to hate.

The barn in which the bats dwelt was haunted by a feral felid that snapped up any pups that fell from the rafters and even swatted adults right out of the air. In a bid for status, the flying squirrel swooped down on the cat to be martyred on behalf of the Chiropterans.

Group identity is a mindless fiction that robs us of autonomy.

Tribes

In the great class of mammalian vertebrates, antagonism arose between the egg-laying monotremes and the marsupials. Neither side could see the other on its own terms, each insisting it was the True Mammal.

An opossum (*Didelphis*) complained, "The platypus is a shameful pretender! It won't admit that it is a failed duck, a builder of nests and hatcher of puggles, unable to fly!"

For its part, the platypus (*Ornithorhynchus*) sought revenge on the marsupials by sowing doubt about their child-rearing abilities:

"We've seen the opossum abandon its newborn babies at birth! The poor things are doomed to forage for a nipple and live in a pocket!"

Steady misrepresentation is the chief hazard of tribal membership.

The Builders

First trees were felled—cottonwood, willow, aspen—and the squirrels came down with them, right in their drays; and the owls and woodpeckers fled their cavities.

Up and down the shore of the brook, trees were gnawed down to stumps, their root systems sprouting dense coppices of sucker wood.

Then the real alterations were begun: branches, rocks, moss, and mud were gathered up and carried or floated downstream then pressed into great, chaotic heaps by the working beavers (*Castor canadensis*), as they had been doing for millennia.

It was extraordinary the way they could lock water into ponds hectares in size; and flood and kill all the standing trees and shrubs; and exile warm-blooded creatures from their dens and burrows, the elegant foxes, the flamboyant skunks, the ground-nesting birds.

No amount of wailing and gnashing of teeth from these victims made a dent in the beavers' preemptive strategy. But when the edges of their pond encroached on the fields and rental properties of the flat-faced ape, beavers were hauled dead out of icy holes on the ends of chains, and their pelts were fashioned into hats and coats.

Then their sturdy dam was breached with dynamite, until only a drowned and mud-ruined landscape remained.

What is not raw material to be used at our disposal is an impediment needing to be cleared away.

The Opportunists

"But that's not right," a hominin rejoins, in response to an enumeration of the beaver's disruptive habits. "The beaver is a keystone species. They improve the land they inhabit, creating nesting sites for waterfowl and migratory birds, providing habitat for fish and invertebrates that depend on wetlands and riverbanks, improving water quality and increasing biodiversity wherever they go. They are a help, not a hindrance. Just ask the thousands of species that colonize the beaver ponds and benefit from the beaver's ingenuity."[52]

The rankest opportunists will be hailed benefactors to the extent that other opportunists thrive in their wake.

Don't Pity the Whistle Pig

When the farmer came to these parts in the 1800s, he dropped forests and pulled stumps; cleared fields of stones and built walls with them; raised buildings and barns and populated them. Thus, the land was rendered fit for the whistle pig (*Marmota monax*).

All went well, until the farmer's grandson's tractor tire collapsed a burrow and the hay wagon broke an axle; until the man's wife's tulip buds disappeared from their stems; until the spring peas and strawberries vanished from tables. But by the time these symptoms manifested themselves, it was already too late.

The losses mounted throughout the county, and thus the persecution of the marmot began. The groundhog was derided for its waste, greed, immorality, theft, and vandalism. Guns, traps, bombs, and poisons were bought and sold.

When the traps and guns discharged, killing off the less wary kits and dams, the shier cousins of these groundhogs kept clawing burrows into adjoining areas, where one family became six, and six in short order became thirty-six.

When the bombs went off and woodchucks suffocated in their chambers, they positioned new entrances here and there, and popped up spy holes, and sniffed the air, and fled into the woods.

When the holes were plugged, the distant cousins of these chucks learned to burrow into and under the stone walls, where they promptly set up breeding chambers. They slept winters and emerged in spring to feed on seedlings.

When later farmers covered their beds of broccoli with cloth and grew peppers in sealed greenhouses and set out electric wire and more traps, the woodchuck repaired to the fields and ate dandelions, clover, grubs, and grasshoppers.

Then the descendants of the farmers began mowing their fields and cutting down brush and building subdivisions and letting their dogs run. The whistle pig just stood up and scanned the flat fields and shrieked and ran for cover.

The farmers had moved on, but the marmot had dug in.

What seems profligacy and waste may in fact be a practical redundancy.

81

Not to Be Outfoxed

Under the new regime established by the flat-faced ape, the elegant fox (*Vulpes*) spends considerable time deluding himself that his hunting success is due solely to his own strength and wit.

He is as blind to the changing times and the sheer abundance of food as the flounder is blind to the directions "right" and "left." Never would he bow to Fortune.

So, when this fox comes upon a pile of chicken carcasses—a place in the woods where a farmer has dumped some dead hens and infertile eggs—he hangs around to feed with ease, all the while congratulating himself on what a good nose he has for edible flesh.

As he feeds, he glances around sharply and unconsciously to see if anyone is watching.

Acknowledging contingency injures one's vanity.

A Mole's Insight

The young meadow voles (*Microtus pennsylvanicus*) were both fascinated and repelled by the star-nosed moles (*Condylura cristata*) that occupied the wet sections of the orchard.

These insectivores appeared vole-like at first, but were fatter, and had a terrifying set of claws—and a face that was an animated squid, the mere glance of which sent the rodents reeling back into their tunnels.

The voles exchanged nightmare visions of tentacled mole attacks, until their elders reminded them that the moles were not enemies, but harmless, and nearly blind as well.

Spying on a mole that had come to the surface to scout out minute arthropods in the mud with its nose tentacles, one vole remarked to the other, "It's a pity to see such a creature deprived of sight, floundering about in the landscape."

The other added, "How can such a being survive?" They simply could not detect the multitudes of tiny creatures the mole was devouring before their very eyes.[53]

Overhearing them, the mole answered, "I am so adapted that, the scales having fallen completely from my eyes, I can apprehend the world the way it is. You, on the other hand, seem preoccupied by phantom shadows, and glare."

Thanatosis

While feeding beyond the orchard stone wall, a *Microtus* made a startling discovery of the horrors of the wild. The vole scurried back down the tunnel to report its finding to its nest mates:

"We all know the pointy-faced 'possum, a hideous creature that nonetheless never harms anyone. A bear happened by, and the mere sight of it shocked the poor 'possum so much it went into a spiral dance and collapsed. But the bear wasn't interested in 'possum, and it merely glanced at the inert creature and moved along. The 'possum lay there with a still grin, foam on its lips, emitting the odor of death. The rugged lynx showed up next to sniff at it, but this lynx was well-fed and turned up its nose at the carrion and continued into the woods. I expected the 'possum to get away, but its immobility now attracted the scavengers![54] As the sky darkened with buzzards circling, I said, 'Why don't you rise?' But it wouldn't budge. It was then I realized the poor 'possum must take itself as given, not as it might wish it were."

Fodder for the Corvid

A cruising corvid spies the elegant *Vulpes* loping along below with the leg of a hen clamped in its jaws, a prize gleaned from the apes' trash dump.

When the fox stops to get a better purchase on the rancid bone, the crow touches down nearby and says, "Ack! The stench!"

The fox pauses in its gnawing to take in the crow's calumny.

"Did you bring down that hen yourself," the corvid goes on, "or have you dogs now adapted yourselves to the slime of apes?"

The fox lunges and snaps at the crow. The corvid simply pirouettes, springs at the bone, and—the reeking quarry now in her own beak—lofts over the head of the incensed fox.

Invective, well-wielded, charms like flattery.

Alpha Male

In his territory of scrawny trees, a chimpanzee (*Pan troglodytes*) moves in on a female stranger nursing her child. She rebuffs him, screaming, "I'm a mother, you beast!"

So, the chimp rips the infant from her arms.

The father of the baby shows up to berate the attacker, "Release our flesh and blood!"

So, the chimp breaks the infant's neck.

Both parents set upon the chimp, yanking his fur and striking his face. "You are unworthy of life!" they yell.

The chimp uses the limp baby as a bludgeon to beat off his assailants.

The mother leaps up and down, wailing, while the father curses the murderer and claws at him.

The chimp retires with the dead infant to the top of the tallest tree to eat in peace.[55]

The surest cure for culpability is the conviction that one's victims had it coming.

The Untamed Shrew

Its sleep having been consumed by nightmares of famine, the short-tailed shrew (*Blarina brevicauda*) rushes off to its newest feeding, ere its pin eyes have even had time to adjust their focus. Devouring a squirming earthworm fat with dirt, the shrew is already sniffing out its next meal, a leopard frog, even while plotting how to poison the naïve vole in the orchard.

In this way, the shrew devours its day, in an endless round of heart-fluttering desperation, culminating in fitful naps and yet more disturbed dreams. It is a poor animal that never has time to enjoy this quivering, dainty thing called life.

An untamed appetite is its own curse.

In a Rut

In rutting season, two mule deer bucks (*Odocoileus hemionus*) settled on unmitigated opposition as the only answer to their standoff: Some decisions in nature must be forced.

As the prize doe grazed nearby, the bucks faced off, horns lowered, hoping to bring a quick end to that which was intolerable to them both. Sometimes one must eliminate an opponent to help oneself to what one wants. But this time it was not to be.

They clashed and snorted through chaparral; slid and tumbled down gullies; slipped and plashed in streams, their antlers interlocking permanently, until one buck became ensnared with the other. They rolled and grunted in the dust, exhausted, but could not extricate themselves from their hateful embrace. The question became not who wins the doe, but who starves first, who breaks whose neck?

A pack of canids showed up that night to make the call: They disemboweled the weaker of the two bucks, allowing the surviving stag to stand up with his foe's decapitated head still attached to his rack. He stumbled off, while the canids feasted on his victim's remains.

Thus, our buck lives on, with his stinking trophy—now only hide and skull—adorning his brow; his prize, the doe in estrus, having long since fled.

Unchecked contention truncates that which it strives for.

Mother's Instinct

A baboon retrieved her baby from the grass, where a hungry felid had dropped it after being hounded by other members of the troop.

Her companion, whose infant fed off her incessantly, observed: "Your baby doesn't eat."

"She is satiated," the mother said. "It means I have fed her well."

Later, these baboons put their infants down in the sunlight to groom them. Struggling to get the parasites off her squirming baby, the one baboon said to the other, "Your baby doesn't move while you groom her."

"She knows how to be patient," the other said. "That way, I can groom her well."

That evening, the flies were particularly awful around the baboon with the inert baby.

"There are so many flies," her companion said. "How can you stand it?"

"There are flies everywhere, always. What can it matter?"

The next morning, the baboon with the squalling baby determined to abandon the mother and the inert baby.

"We can no longer bear your child's awful smell!"

"That is why I keep her close. I do not notice so much anymore."

Elegy for a Sciurid

To the gray squirrel (*Sciurus carolinensis*), it seems the scrubby, well-rifled forest floor just gives way to nothing. There is gravel and filthy piles of snow, that is all, no vegetation. It is the end of the world.

The squirrel hops out into the middle of this wasteland, in puzzlement, and flexes his tail. It undulates like a banner. The ground is the barest bone now, a flat, featureless surface, but at least it has some warmth.

Pawing around, sniffing, he sits back on his haunches and tries to get his bearings. He can see trees across the way, in what looks like a distant country.

A noise encroaches: Instantly, the squirrel thinks, "Predator!" and darts off in one direction, feints, and switches back—only to be crushed by two tires in succession.

Under new conditions of life, adaptive talents are rendered suddenly obsolete.

CHAPTER FIVE
The Rise of Homo

The Ape with a Voice in His Head

Not articulate speech. Urges and grunts, rather. Inclinations manifest as emotional noise.[56] The notions of this flat-faced, long-legged beast might be rendered thus:

"Hunter, get the hell off my foot!"

"Ma'am, it is simply out of courtesy that I give you this meat."

And: "Secret? What secret?"

In time, such sentiments could be put on the air and wafted over to a neighbor, piecemeal, incoherently at first, but with reiteration finally honed to true speech. Thus, they learned to carry each other around in their heads, and they could contemplate their neighbor the way one contemplates one's own face in a puddle. It could be whispered: "Doth thy neighbor love thee or hate thee?"

They found they could doctor the impressions of themselves that others carried around, fashion faces as they pleased, with just a flick of the tongue. Some mistook this deception for complete self-creation, as if their animal nature had ceased to exist, but this was the worst of deception of all. Yet, the truth often came out in their fables:

> *The monkey with nothing hid in the bushes and roared like a lion.*
> *When the others fled, he took everything for himself.*[57] *So watch out.*

After Their Kind

With the arrival of words, these new great apes began to stratify themselves, assigning titles to positions of command and epithets to those who followed. The destitute clumped together in disparate settlements, while the lucky few dwelled in the highlands. Some accumulated hides and tools, others lovers and children, still others stories and legends. All spoke, ate, and dressed according to type. But type turned out to be mostly a fib.

A worm, begotten in the guts of invader tribes and released into flowing streams, took up residence in the guts of these new hominins, indiscriminately—and the people developed fever, chills, weakness, dysentery, until finally they collapsed and died. Those left standing wandered about, dazed, wondering what had spared them. They examined leaves and stars for reasons, but there seemed to be no moral to the story.

A few who had accumulated lovers and offspring managed to persist. They spread through the valleys and interbred with the invaders, until their kind disappeared forever.

Mayhem

A confluence of rooks (*Corvus*) and waxwings (*Bombycilla*), compounded by the presence of a predatory *Buteo* hawk nearby, stirred up such a disturbance in a Pleistocene spring woodland that even the flat-faced ape paused in its work to take notice.

This amused ape—a thick, stumpy specimen seated on its duff— looked away from the clamor and continued its task, dashing one fat rock against another, until fragments broke off and hit the bare ground.

The waxwings swarmed in twittering masses around the roosting rooks which, one-by-one, merely flapped away, lofting themselves higher into the branches of the fir trees. There they encountered the watchful *Buteo*, and immediately they began to shriek in horror.

The rooks' sudden departure from the treetops sent the waxwings scattering like tossed gravel; but they doubled back and, thinking better of open flight, settled deeper into the trees.

The rooks shouted insults at the hawk, who merely moved over to another branch. This was not to the satisfaction of either the rooks or the waxwings—and on the clamor went.

The rhythmic *clack, clack* of the ape pounding stones together was enough to draw the birds' attention away from their squabbling, into momentary silence.

They turned to watch as a taller, more attenuated ape strode out of the woods. It stood over the stone-working ape and watched it a moment. Then it stooped over to pick up a stone chip, glanced at it, tossed the chip away; it picked up another chip, tossed it away. The squat ape stopped clacking stone against stone and watched his thinner counterpart toss all his work away. He then resumed his clacking, more intensely now, even furiously. More chips struck the ground.

The tall ape turned fiercely on the squat one; he seized the rock in the other's fist and wrenched it from him. The other began to cry out, which sounded to the birds like pure agony.

The tall one raised the pilfered stone and chucked it into the woods, sending the other into paroxysms of noise. The stone-

93

bereft ape followed the tall one into the woods, both their tongues wagging wildly. The noise scared the hawk away.

One rook observed to the other, "Such a racket these apes make."

His cohort responded, "They do that, you know."

Their quarrel with the hawk had ended.

Mammoth Hunters

When the ice relented prematurely, and the cold rains had cleansed the fields of snow, the woolly *Mammuthus* found it could graze much earlier than usual in areas it had never been able to graze in before.[58] The spruce and pine forests looked particularly dark and grim but were putting on a formidable green through the cold fog. The herd delighted in the early pastures and lingered below the walls of the glacier.

The burgeoning season tempted intruder hominins north as well. They emerged from the woods like ants and streamed toward the herd, their animal-hide coverings looking black in the dreary, late winter light. Bristling with wooden spears, they stirred up thunder and trumpets.

One mammoth tripped and went down—an elderly, slower male—but the rest got away, grateful for the anonymity of the herd.

The early stages of an endgame always look manageable.

The Hunter's Version

The flat-faced, long-legged ape tells the story of the mammoth hunt this way:

"The gods guided the tips of our spears into the mammoth because we had dipped them into clear waters. Otherwise the mammoth's hide would have deflected our points like flies."

His son asked, "How did the mammoth come to be in such a position to be speared in the first place?"

"Its spirit had abandoned it. It must have offended the gods somehow. This allowed us to divide it from the herd."

"How was the herd found in these parts at this time of year?"

"They found ground forage out of season, for the gods had made the ice yield."

"Of what interest is it to the gods to make the ice yield?"

"What a silly question! To make the mammoths more accessible to us! The gods thereby secure for themselves our fragrant sacrifices."

Narrative is an infirmity that causes us to see history as a set of myths rather than as a continuum of lucky breaks.

The Theater

The boy discovered that soft charcoal leaves a mark when pressed against hard stone and that the black color looks good against the background of the gray stone.

With this method, he forced into view his version of the mammoth hunt. The figure evoked the great spirit of the mammoth itself to all that saw it.

The tribe gathered around and marveled at it, reenacting amongst themselves the story the stone told.

Then the rains came and washed it all away.

It happened several times this way, the boy retelling on stone the story of the mammoth hunt and everyone getting animated, until the rains came.

A priestess recognized that something special was at play here. She took the boy aside and told him of a place where he could reproduce the mammoth hunt and no element could sully his story, ever.

The boy scrambled along with her through passages in the dark earth that were so narrow he thought he would die. But at last the priestess brought him into a chamber where the fire-lit walls never saw rain.

In our hunt for permanence, we court the inaccessible.

The Lesson

Using vines and the meager light thrown off a fatty wick, the boy managed to lower himself, and a girl, down into the rock chamber, to view his work.

There, on the scraped rock surface—between one ancestor's ibex and another's auroch—stood his mammoth, noble in outline, awaiting its death.

Recognizing what she was seeing, the girl was moved to silence. Then she said, "The hunters say you draw the mammoth here to ensure the survival of the herd. Is that why you have drawn it?"

"That might be why a hunter would draw it," the boy answered.

The girl said, "The priestess says you have drawn the mammoth to make peace with its ancestors. Is that why you have drawn it?"

"That might be why a priestess would draw it."

"The medicine man says –"

"The medicine man knows nothing, neither."

"Then why come down here and draw it?"

"Because," the boy said. "It is my favorite beast." He picked up a rolled-up scrap of hide. "What is your favorite?"

He showed her how to hold the hide roll against the wall and drag pigment over the rock.

She took it, thought a moment, then traced the way her flesh curved first one way then curved the other way. Then she drew concentric portals leading into the womb.[59]

The execution was realistic enough to cause them both to giggle.

Competence that lingers is its own reward.

Wild Boars

A destitute hominin ventured out of its domain to scour up a meal in the woods, but he had to scramble up a tree to escape the tusks of some feral pigs seemingly bent on revenge.

"It wasn't me personally who ate your kind!" pled the ape.

"And it wasn't us personally your fathers slaughtered," replied the boars, "but the appetite for your flesh hasn't left us."

In nature, food and foe are relative terms.

Rhinoceros, Run

With fire brands and enough hands, the tribe could compel a herd of woolly rhinoceroses[60] (*Coelodonta antiquitatis*) to do what they wanted. The elder brother in charge knew the trick was allowing the animals to run free, to let them believe they were making a clean escape. It was a simple, if wasteful strategy.

The younger brother, though, was a dreamer. "We should hunt the rhinoceros as we do the fish," he said, "selectively, with a pointed barb, a harpoon."

His brother laughed. "A rhinoceros would break your harpoon like a fiber."

"Not if we made it out of the rhinoceros' horn!"

"That's clever," said the elder, "but why bother?"

That evening, they drove the rhinoceroses off a cliff.

Abundance contains the seed of its own undoing.

Hosannas

A young hominin and his father are out hunting frogs by a pond. They are far away from the tribe, where they can feel surrounded by just the trees and speak to one another without fear of being overheard.

As they wait for the mist to depart from the waters, they hear wild toms erupting along the woods margins, a clamorous chorus.

"I wonder what they're saying," the boy says.

"They are arguing over whose god's the sacred one," Dad answers. "Even though they are brothers who court the same hens, they cannot agree on the proper display of feathers, whether it is fit to eat seeds or insects, or even what the deity's name is."

"Silly birds!" the boy says. "What is wrong with them?"

"They know of no better way to impress the hens."

How to Best the Vicious Stoat

The mother was mute and could not console her grieving child. She wiped the tears from the girl's face and then picked up an egg.

With one of her porcupine quill tools she carefully demonstrated how to pierce the shell on the narrow end. She then turned the egg around and did the same to the fat end, passing the quill all the way through the egg, until she could draw the quill out the first hole. She then put the egg to her lips and blew hard, ejecting the contents into a small clay bowl.

She mixed poison with the yolk in the bowl, then piped it all back into the empty egg, using a hollow quill to blow it in. She sealed the two holes in the egg with clay and buried it in the ashes beneath the fire.

After a few hours, the mother woke the child from a slumber and placed the cooled egg in her hand.

Imitation is the means for having things our own way.

Poet Ape

Amid the hominins arose a poet, a gregarious young female, a complier of words. Her mother was the tribe's lead gatherer and herbalist, one who knew the secret haunts of plants that others did not know.

The girl had recently studied the tongue of the hairy woods folk. She recited her inventory of words to her mother as they foraged together. "Like us, they call their babies 'kids', their ancestors 'souls', and their husbands 'bucks'."

"Then they stole it from us," her mother concluded, uprooting a fat bulb, then giving thanks with a perfunctory prayer.

"But they even chant their thanks for food, just as you do."

"Don't be ridiculous, child. That would mean we were kin with the woods folk. Everyone knows those flesh-eaters are animals."

Dog-Eat-Ape World

A canid captive since it was a pup had learned to distinguish between the tribeswomen and the tribesmen, and even tribe from tribe. It heeled and cringed in the presence of the hairy woods folk and tore into the flesh of the herbalists. It came down to a matter of smell—these apes all basically tasted the same—and the dog was not fooled by this particular ape's pretense of superiority over other apes.

So, when the keeper goaded the dog into attacking an herbalist that had wandered onto tribal territory, and then stood back to observe the ensuing mayhem, shouting, "Good dog!", the canid reminded the ape:

"I am but a proxy for your own savage instincts which, like us dogs, are cultivated and deployed at will."

Hunter's Fancy

When the young hunter came of age, his mother clapped for joy upon seeing the red hairs sprouting from the boy's chin.

"Ha!" she cried. "You've received the same blessing as your grandfather before you!"

"It is just red hair," he said.

"But a blessing, nonetheless. ... Long ago, an ancestral hunter of yours, whose family languished from lack of meat, vowed to eat nothing but raw berries until the gods relented and granted him game. They subsisted on the berries until the berries were gone, and then they ate fire ants. They fed on fire ants until the fire ants were gone. Then they ate red clay, and the clay never gave out. When they stood up in the sun, their hair shone like copper! The gods were so impressed they showered them with birds and rabbits. That's how you've come from a line of successful hunters."

"Where did you get all this?" the boy asked.

"Directly from your grandfather," she answered.

"And where did he get it?"

"Why, from his own grandfather, of course!"

Fancy, like hair color, is an inheritance.

Stone Age

Around a spent cooking fire, picking flesh from their teeth, two elders and their minions thought deeply about the skirmish of late that had diminished them. As usual—and alas! —there were two schools of thought:

"It would seem the warriors were too cavalier in their comments about the women," the first elder asserted.

"But only after the women had foraged on sacred hunting ground," the second noted.

The first elder shook his head. "You, too, a disparager of women!"

"You would permit them to place their filthy feet in a field where men toil?"

"Slanderer!" the first shouted. "It was a field of stones! Of what use are they?"

"Sacrilege!" Standing up from the fire, the second elder demonstrated his point with a stone to the other's skull.

Causes of war are not to be discovered, only pretexts.

Horse and Rider

The horse has learned to be calm with the long-legged ape clinging to its back. This took some time, but the ape was a parasite that would not let go. This symbiosis spawned wars of expansion, and the horse became universal.

Now, it is like it has always been this way, *Homo* and *Equus* conquering the Earth together, and the horse has let go of all its old fables of the steppes and its vicious carnivores.

There is one thing about the horse, though: When the ape is done with it for the day, slipping off the lines and releasing it into its enclosure, the horse kicks up its hooves and farts in the ape's face, enacting a little satire of its previous, liberated state.

We are convinced of free will to the extent that the circumscription is invisible.

Beards

The men of the tribe grew long beards that were striking to behold. They teased and dyed and tweaked, so that the women became transfixed by what they saw. To enhance the effect, the men braided the hair and wove in twigs, feathers, and fungi, and created ornaments out of spiders and roaches. Youths were given gifts of combs at puberty, and old men fragrant oil treatments on their deathbeds. Myths grew up around bearding. It was said that the idea came down from their forebears, the bison, who had taught the first man how to copulate with a woman.

And so, the tribe became convinced that, should a hair on a man's face ever be shorn, his male descendants would shrivel and die within himself. Then a woman gave birth to a boy who, after an uneventful childhood hunting birds and lizards, grew up to have no hair on his face. After his father perished in battle, his kinfolk waited to promote the boy, holding back the ceremonial comb for a pubescence which never seemed to arrive.

Yet he grew tall and strong and was able to overcome the taunts and pinches of the hairy boys:

"What are you, a woman?"

"The shame of your father!"

"If he were alive, he would slay you."

The young women, it turned out, were amazed by the smooth youth. He loomed tall in their dreams, like a lean horse running among woolly mammoths.

Soon the beardless youth was fathering children with other men's wives. In retaliation, the cuckolds wrestled him to the ground and held a bone knife to his genitals.

"You have no beard to cut off, so what are we supposed to do?"

Rugged illusions mask flimsy beliefs.

Feathered Friends

In their dealings with them, the herbalists noticed that the hairy woods folk had taken to wearing in their hair the dark feathers of gallinaceous birds and corvids. The arrangements were varied and exquisite, in configurations that the herbalists were unable to decipher in terms of their own codes of dress.

This prompted them to wonder, "Will they next begin squawking like crows, or perhaps clucking like hens?" They knew it best to conduct trade with the feather-encrusted folk stone-faced, in order to ensure the free flow of goods from them—hide vessels, gut cord, and bone needles—even though they could barely contain their laughter.

One wag herbalist wove found feathers and debris into her hair in an obvious parody of her neighbors' custom. These included the tiny primary feathers of songbirds dropped on the path, down from abandoned nests, along with rattling seed pods and bright fungi.

It became a sensation amongst the young to thus mock their neighbors and scandalize their elders.

"Look at yourselves, will you?" the elders observed. "You look like cannibals."

"What do you mean?" the young laughed. "We ate no birds!"

A Savage Courtship

The hairy woodsman said to his brother, "The darling herbalist doesn't notice me, even though I parade around with my hunting axe."

"She's not impressed by your axe," his brother told him, "for she is a widow, her husband having died in the skirmish of late."

So, the smitten woodsman trapped fur animals and used his axe to chop them apart. He fashioned a cape from the coats of elegant foxes and wrapped himself in it.

When he next saw his brother, he said, "The darling herbalist still never even glances at me, though I wear this mantle of the finest fur."

"She's not impressed by your furs," his brother said, "for she is the mother of boys and has given life rather than caused death."

Undaunted, the love-sick woodsman chased down a large ungulate, chopped off the buck's horns and wore them on his own head as sorcerers do.

"She's laughing at you!" his brother said. "Her eldest boy is a warrior, like his father before him, one who was wounded defending his father in the skirmish of late."

One day, the woodsman crossed paths with the adolescent warrior. He pulled out his axe and, with three terrible blows to the back of the cervical spine, chopped off the boy's head.

"He looked me in the eye!" the woodsman protested.

At the wedding ceremony, a dove was incinerated in honor of the bride's warrior-son.

Raven Feathers

While out scouting fungi, an herbalist came across the body of one of the hairy woods folk, a fallen warrior left to succumb to a spear wound.

The herbalist knew just what to do: She gathered up fragrant leaves, made a poultice of them, and stuffed his mouth full. She arranged the warrior's body in the proper attitude, covered him with a carnivore's hide, and summoned her tribesmen to fetch him.

The woods folk were grateful for the return of their warrior's remains and for the respect that the herbalist had lavished upon them.

For the commemoration ceremony, the herbalist was given a special invitation. She decided to hold her nose and attend. Her elders told her to eat no ceremonial flesh.

There in the woods, the folk presented the herbalist with the prestigious Plume of Gratitude. She added it to her already-impressive headdress of feathers.

With good deeds we plume our reputations.

Fertility

A young gatherer became smitten with a hairy boy, one of the woods folk. Stumbling out of the woods, burrs and stick-tights adorning her hair and tunic, her arms laden with small white flowers, she declared to her sisters, "He is a god!"

But the girls would not hear of it. "She has her eye on an animal! What can we do?" They broke open tree stems and read them, and cast torn leaves into the wind, studying their scatter patterns.

One of the sisters suddenly smiled with an idea. She spent days tracking the boy, just as her sister would. When she saw him squatting near a stream, she made a mental note of it and returned to the place later in the day. There she found what she was looking for, scooped it into a small basket with a stick, and took it to her sisters to inspect.

They howled in delight. "This will teach her he is no god!"

Next time the girl showed up, disheveled with lust, the sisters presented the basket to her, saying, "Look what your hairy boyfriend left in the woods for you! Some god!"

She took the basket, uncovered it, and stared into it with one eye closed. "Thank you," she said, closing the basket and tucking it into her tunic. "With this will I fertilize the flower of my love."

Therianthrope

On the day of remembrance, an ancestral spirit pranced into the village, all horns and balls and fur, but upright, on two legs, rattling its rattle.[61] The children shrieked and ran away clapping their hands to keep at bay other creatures that may be swarming about. The border between worlds seemed rent open to them. Anything might appear now, even death.

The beast danced a familiar dance to still their fears, then asked them each in succession if they knew the creature's identity.

"You are an inhabitant of the world beyond rock," said one boy.

"You come from the land of the grandfathers," said another.

"Yes." The beast rattled its rattle. "The world under the ground. The grandfathers of you all."

One girl was not having any of it. "You are no grandfather," she shouted. "You are only half a man and half of an animal!"

"No, child." The beast stood before the girl. "I am *all* of an animal." The eyes, hair, and teeth indeed said so. But the sorceress then doffed her hood of horns: "But I'm half-human—" With her free hand, she cupped her ceremonial balls, two heavy stones in a leathern sack— "and half-bull!"

Pure Smoke

When the herbalist gatherers discovered how fire worked to liberate healing plant life from the Earth, they realized just what hairy savages the woods folk were.

The top sorcerer gave due thanks to the leaves and stars for this insight. "Witness how they seduce our daughters," he said, "and snatch them away. Witness the corruption of our youth, who now think it proper to look like animals. All this while we struggle to maintain cleanliness."

He got together a party of gatherers to touch fire to the entrance of the woods folk's forest, just to smoke them out. But the dry leaves quickly spread the rumor that the unclean were about to be swept from the Earth.

The woods folk released their dogs and rained arrows down on the herbalists, but a wave of flame drove them back, and finally to extinction.

Later, when fragrant annual plants and woody herbs began to repopulate the scorched ground, the sorcerer interpreted it as a sign of righteousness.

Last True Hunter

This hunter hunted as no other. Sprinting doubled over in tall grass, he got near enough to his quarry to dart it. When the shaft broke off the poisoned arrow, he retrieved it and secured it in his quiver.[62]

He and his fellows tracked the targeted beast for days while the poison took effect. They studied the tracks of beetles and birds that had scurried across the beast's footprints, and they noted how the beast's urine stains had darkened as it fled deeper into bush country.

When at last they came upon the beast hiding in a thicket, they knew it would charge them ere it died. As the beast lifted itself out of the dust and made a final challenge, the hunter knelt with his spear to pierce its heart.

They promptly sliced the beast into strips, which they slung over carrying poles. Then they ate the beast's liver so that they had the energy to sing during the long hike back to the encampment.

Upon seeing the clump of men returning from the hunt, the tribe's people clapped and shouted. At last, they would have meat.

Back at camp, the hunter presented the shaft of the poisoned arrow to the boy who had entrusted him with it, and to his mother. They would see to it that the meat was passed out fairly.

Freed from the burden of having to decide how the prize should be distributed, the hunter returned to the task of digging grubs to extract poison for newer darts.

Farmer Ape

A gatherer in this period would usually be headed over the horizon to scrounge up the nuts and berries that sustained the family. But this gatherer was tired.

He had heard the dark rumors. So, behind his dwelling he cleared a spot of stones and plants. He buried the seeds of cereals one by one, at regular intervals, like words in a chant, and waited.

When the rains let up, the others wondered what he was still doing on this side of the horizon. Shoots emerged, and the planter minded them; and before anyone became aware of what he was doing, the fragrant meadow of the wild had gathered at his abode.

There was just one man in the village older than he, and it was this one who confronted him:

"You have failed us! By wrenching the seed from the field, you threaten to wrench all men from Nature and force them to stay at their abodes with their wives."[63]

The villagers trampled the man's crop into the dirt and burned his dwelling to the ground.

To prove the violence of such wrenching, they hacked open his chest and brought out his heart for him to see for himself.

The Innovators

An early farmer was disgusted by the long drought—his people's grains stood starkly on the bone-white flats and would not grow—so in disobedience of the local gods he fashioned a wall out of sticks and diverted a stream with it.

The grains revived, panic was averted, and the farmer was showered with accolades and speaking engagements.

At one such event, an angry resident from downstream confronted him:

"You have stolen for yourselves what the gods have created for us all. What shall we do now that the waters have ceased flowing in our land and our children wail with hunger?"

"Move," the farmer suggested.

Those inconvenienced by innovation are seldom if ever countenanced.[64]

The Mighty Milker

The grain-eaters of the little village panicked as the mighty *Bos* was led into the square on the end of a line.

Peering from behind corners and jugs, they watched as the keeper clucked to the auroch and brought her to heel. Could this truly be the beast of the field, or was it a phantom?

They came forth one by one, to behold and to touch. It certainly smelled like a beast, and it bellowed as in the wild, but she did not turn her horns against the man or try to escape him. How could this be?

He told them he had stolen her as a calf from her mother and raised her as his own child. He talked to her daily and was responsible for her provender. He even selected the bull to be her mate.

He requested a vessel, and when it was brought to him, he crouched with it and brought streams of milk from the bovid's udders with his bare hands.

Yes, this must be a phantom, surely the work of the gods.

Then suddenly, the auroch turned and let loose a stream of green-brown shit that spattered on the cobblestones and drizzled down her shanks.

The villagers scattered; and they knew then that the keeper truly had a beast on his hands.

A Pastoral Parable

On the barren slopes live the shepherds. Those in the valleys below raise swine.

The herders are seasonal: they wander with the herds of sheep. From the hills, they can look down on the swineherds below.

"How loathsome the sedentary life is, living deep in the clefts of the hills," sniffs one shepherd to another. "Their livestock live amongst their dwellings, shitting in the same place, day after day! That is the definition of unclean."

His companion adds, "Look how even their children's noses turn up at the end."

Meanwhile, the swineherds espy the herders haunting the outskirts, like feral beasts. One swineherd remarks to another, "You can smell those shepherds coming a league away."

"Yes," rejoins the other, "and if you had to haul your livestock around with you, everywhere you go, day and night—even to sleep!—why, you'd stink, too."

Familiarity is no guarantor of toleration.

Accidental Medicine

When the tribe of herders married off their daughter to a tribe of gatherers, they brought their herds with them to the ceremony. This was a solemn occasion, as the herders had had no success intermarrying with other tribes in the area: The subsequent generations always died off, and the herders acquired a reputation for being cursed.

This was because, unknown to everyone present, invisible herds of spirochetes[65] always trailed in with them during the nuptials.

This new group—who eschewed all meat—was adamant that no unclean thing be permitted within the sacred ceremonial circle: The herders had to check their herds at the door, no matter how well-groomed they were.

Given the bride's tribe's appalling record, the top herbalists among the gatherers doubled their unique concoctions, consisting of honey and sour fruits, bitter bark, and pungent herbs. They prayed that the curse be held at bay.

They chanted around the woman and anointed her. She professed her allegiance to the herbalists, and she vowed that her children would eat no unclean thing. Her parents wept.

With the bride thus converted, the spirochetes died out, and the new line persisted.

Culture is the means by which the ape outstrips natural selection.

Horse Trader

After working a wild steed to the point that its splints were stressed, with no effect on the animal's intransigent nature, the pastoralist decided he needed to be rid of it. First, he consulted a trusted herbalist to come up with a suitable concoction—some slow-acting, unobtrusive poison—to calm the ungovernable beast. Then he tried to snag a buyer.

He approached a trader passing through the village on his way east, one who had said he needed new legs under himself to get there. The pastoralist said he had just the set of legs for him.

After he had supplemented the steed's fodder with leaves and flowers the herbalist had prescribed, he was able to lead it on the end of a line out into the square, where it stood like an obedient child. The trader was impressed and gave him gold.

Several leagues outside of the territory, the steed, with the trader on its back, began to contort its neck, whinny, and come down hard on its forelegs. The trader used his knees and lines to try to bring the horse under control, but it was apparent this beast did not understand control.

Not knowing where it was, the horse threw off its rider and bolted into the desert. It fell down and began to roll in the dust, as if it had a wild cat clinging to its back. Then it died.

A passing traveler, who helped bind the fallen man's wounds, said he knew of the pastoralist who had sold the horse, back in the territory.

"His reputation is as stained as his teeth," he said. "You know what they say, 'Let the buyer beware.'"

The traveler showed his savior a shard of pelvic bone, taken from a fallen warrior, the tip of which fit like a pike between the fingers of his right hand.

"Rather, let the seller die," he said.

The Tablet

Leave it to the farmer to instruct the earth to talk to him, to seize on a chunk of clay and confide in it his sense of aggrievement, itemize the deficiencies of his neighbors.

The neighbors were incredulous. "What fable does your little slab tell you today?" they smirk.

The farmer gazes at the flat face of the tablet in his palm, brushes the tips of his fingers down the many scores that craze the surface, and says, "As the gods tell us, it is the nature of Appetite to outstrip Means. So, when a citizen owes another a sheep but can't afford to pay it back, let him go back to eating porridge."

A neighbor wrenches the clay fragment from the farmer's hand and glares at it. Its surface is nonsense, the peck marks of jackdaws. He pitches the tablet to the ground and stomps on it till it breaks.

"What do the gods say now?"

No creation is so well wrought that it cannot be undone in a stroke.

The Savage

As if it were not bad enough that the landowner had clapped members of the neighboring tribe into the yoke, he pitted them against one another in contests of endurance until they collapsed into heaps at the end of the day. Then he had them sing songs of praise to him, tunes he had written himself, and prance about in their bonds like work horses. They were paid for their entertainments with the very fodder they had been enslaved to grow.

One of the landowner's sons marveled at this arrangement. "How can you stand to witness, let alone celebrate the suffering you cause?"

"They are but apes," his father said. "They don't feel as we do."

Savagery commences from ignorance of our own animal nature.

What the Priestess Said

The slave owner's son took himself to the tower of the village priestess, whose impressive disguise consisted of crows' feathers, bear hides and sharks' teeth.

"Am I doomed to play the role my fathers have written for me?" the son anguished.

"Your fathers never wrote it," the Priestess said.

"It is a life of dominance and cruelty and paranoia," the son said.

"You could be the one in bonds," the Priestess said.

The son was despondent. "Who would devise such a fiendish existence?"

The priestess guided the son's eyes outward and upward from the tower. "It is written in the stars," she said, with a sweeping hand. "They are beyond our understanding."

Belief facilitates savagery under the guise of higher authority.

Holy Man

During the famine, the old holy man appeared before the priestess dressed in a dyed flowing gown, a braided beard that hung to his waist, a crown of leaves and flowers adorning his pate.

He chewed on his ceremonial nut and spat ritually before he spoke. "Go to the settlement and bring the children of the starving to me."

The priestess went to the settlement and met little resistance when she asked for the children. In fact, their mothers wept upon hearing their babies would be fed.

The priestess rounded up the children and brought them up the mountain to the holy man's cave, where they were promptly fed and clothed.

Once contented, the children picked up charcoal from the floor and began marking up the walls of the cave.

The priestess wrenched the charcoal from their little hands.

The holy man spat and said, "No. Let them draw their animal spirits upon these walls."

The cave soon became a diorama, with big eating little, and bigger still chasing after the big.

The priestess taught the children the names and relationships of all creatures. The holy man spat out fabulous lies about their origins.

None of them knew that the priestess and the holy man knew nothing.

In this way, the holy man maintained a plentiful stock of children to be offered to the gods.

Ostentatious displays often advertise what one is not.

Insignia of Warriors

The tribe's men—in their pursuit to discover some pretext for separating their neighbors from their fat livestock—took off their reed skirts and stole naked into the woods, for they did not want to risk making any sound and being detected. Painted to the highest order of invisibility with their mystery dyes, crouching from tree to tree, they were able to privately scout out the neighboring warriors' ceremony to bring back to their wives news of their abutters' barbarism.

They glimpsed young men dancing in fire light—not just showing off their spears but their members! These men had scarified the whole lengths of their penises, the scars joining up with a web of scars along their flat abdomens. And—most horribly—they had pulled their foreskins forward, stretched them like anteaters' snouts, and clasped them shut at the end with bone ornaments.

This last feature turned the stomachs of the spies, inducing them to flee back to their village to smear their neighbors: "Not just lacking reed skirts, but pierced and pinioned are these savages—on the tips of their pendulous snoods!" This riled the villagers toward war.

Meanwhile, the chants of the dancing, pierced warriors continued pulsing on the night air. The bold truth, disguised from the other tribe in a foreign tongue, filled their own clan with fervor:

"They hide their shame under grass skirts! They've cut away the better part of themselves with a stone blade and thrown it to dogs!"

Success in cultivating discord entails making the familiar seem strange.

CHAPTER SIX
Homo domesticus

The Worm

When the ape arrives in the land and becomes a farmer, he pulls down trees and plucks out rocks to set up his homestead. Immediately, the Worm plagues him.

Armyworms plow through his turf, wire worms drill into his roots, and earworms bore into his grain. To defeat them, the farmer burns the fields and turns over the soil and plants an orchard.

The Worm graduates to the trees, plaguing them with bark borer and fruit maggot and codling moth. Incensed, the farmer exterminates them with sprays and concoctions, smothering eggs, paralyzing adults.

But the Worm is tireless. It occupies the farmer's livestock, bloating their stomachs, riddling their brains, infecting their eyes. Undaunted, the farmer culls and slaughters and roasts until the Worm is routed.

Then the Worm infests the farmer's children. It inhabits their intestines and resides in their blood. The outraged farmer invents potions that kill the Worm in place. After he purges his children, they inherit the world.

Finally, the farmer is down to one last Worm that dwells in a far corner of his pantry.

"Aha!" the farmer says, before throttling it. "What say you now, Worm?"

"It's a wonder," the Worm says, "your own pestilential nature never offends you."

The Gull

The gull (*Larus canus*) has a way of hovering above the landfill, like a chalky spider hanging from an invisible line, coasting along in search of the detritus of human habitation.

Amidst the heaps of stinking trash, the derelict, flat-faced ape says to the gull, "It's unnatural to see you feeding here when you could find food on the beach."

"Your kind have defiled and denuded the beaches," the gull says. "Here I eat what I want, when I want."

Thus, the gull, which evolved near the salty gyres of ancient seashores, finds itself perfectly at home in this sprawling, heaving wasteland.

It is only natural for the ape to imagine the unnatural.

The Owls' View

The flat-faced, long-legged ape had become a force of nature, like a volcanic archipelago or a plague of locusts.

As the hominins moved into all the hospitable areas of the planet, other species complained. Those affected included ruminant and carnivore alike, who fell victim first to the apes' arrows then to their guns.

The hominins wrenched some species to their wills—like the felids and the canids—while others became collateral damage. Squirrels (*Sciurus*), skunks (*Mephitis*) and weasels (*Mustela*) ended up crushed on road surfaces, and arthropods of all kinds dropped out of fouled skies or sank to the bottoms of dingy seas.

When the din of complaint reached the sensitive, oval faces of some barn owls (*Tyto alba*) dwelling near an orchard, they reacted with amusement.

"It looks to us like the complainers have no problem replenishing their numbers," the owls observed. "Judging by the plentitude of voles as of late, we doubt there is a problem at all."

Foresight entrained to self-interest is obtuse.

Tainted

The hominins did not get on well with their primate neighbors, the baboons, who pawed through the garbage dump and stunk up the area with feces.

The humans were especially offended by the baboons' everyday domestic affairs, deploring their biting, their slapping, and their scuffling. The men were shocked by the females' sexual displays, and the women by the alphas' brutal mating habits.

Without a hint of irony, the humans decided "to be rid of the brutes" and poisoned the baboon troop with contaminated meat scraps laid out for them to find in the dump.

The troop did not get wiped out, however. In a frenzy after the meat, the alphas beat and bit any low-ranking male, female or juvenile who even attempted to go for one of the scraps.

The alphas hoarded the meat for themselves; consequently, only they died of the poison,[66] leaving the rest of the troop unharmed to plague the humans.

The costs of brutality are paid for indirectly.

Cultured

Most of the troop of baboons survived being poisoned by meat tainted by humans in their contempt. Those left behind included all the juveniles and females, and a smattering of low-ranking males, those who preferred grooming others over slapping and biting them.

The females immediately saw this as an opportunity: With the alphas gone, there would be no more brutality, and the females decided to make this permanent.

If an adolescent male newcomer[67] exhibited any tendencies toward self-indulgent violence, the females simply withdrew their attentions and turned their backs on him. Getting on became preferred over getting one's way.

Now the humans, so hopelessly embroiled in their own culture of brutality, despaired of ever matching the baboons for their harmony.

Culture amends the most intractable dispositions.

Philosopher King

A head of state became infected with a protist[68] from a constant diet of red meat, the prerogative of a ruler in a country where such meats are rare. The parasite immediately encysted itself in the ruler's brain, and from there it proceeded to rule the state.

Already bloody-minded, this head of state lost all inhibition. From his mouth flowed invective and intimidation, and when his advisors questioned the wisdom of his speaking thus, he answered, "The honorable king speaks his mind."

The head of state grew careless about bodily protection, sometimes eschewing armor and even wandering out of the ken of his bodyguards. Warned of the danger, he responded, "The well-respected king shows his people he is not afraid."

This ruler began a campaign of unprovoked hazing against his neighbors. When the citizens of the land, conscripted into a cause they did not support, protested, he said, "The competent king preempts before being preempted."

This tyrant developed a whole philosophy of provocation, risk and aggression, by which he amassed adjoining lands, subdued all the people and confiscated their wealth. But the citizenry suffered from the resulting wars and ended up living in poverty and disease.

At last, they rose up, joined forces with their embittered neighbors, and decapitated the head of state.

Reason functions as the barest cortex of action.

Porcupine or Skunk?

Two farmers discuss the relative demerits of pest species.

"The skunk is the worst," says the chicken farmer. "It emerges in the dead of winter from burrows under the sheds and gains access to the coops. There it feasts on eggs and poults, even taking a full-grown chicken now and then. And if you ever tangle with one, so help you God you'll reek for a month."

"Bah. The skunk is a pussycat compared to the porcupine," says the apple grower. "I've had them in my trees, where they denude the bark and chew through branches until they drop off. Then they take one bite out of every single apple. You try to trap them, and they just move to another tree. And if you ever tangle with one, you'll be wishing you reeked for a month."

But the chicken farmer stays true to his hatred of skunks. Then one night a porcupine chews its way into the chicken shed and lets the weasels in.

"I told you," the apple grower says, "the porcupine is a beast."

The apple grower loathes the porcupine above all others. Then some skunks discover the beehives in his orchard and stand at the hives' entrances stuffing their mouths with bees and even knocking over boxes.

"Now you know what a menace the skunk is," says the chicken farmer. The porcupine gets into his tool shed and gnaws the handles of his rakes and shovels; and when his dog tries to catch it, the dog gets a mouthful of quills and dies of infection.

"Nothing beats the porcupine for destruction," says the apple grower.

A skunk claws up his lawn for grubs; and when his dog goes after it, it bites the dog, which contracts rabies.

To experience the balance of nature is to abhor it.

A Model Moose

In the north woods park, against a backdrop of sheer granite, the bull moose (*Alces alces*) steps out of a coniferous wilderness and poses near the shore of an alpine pond.

Several hundred feet away, on the other side of the pond, a group of tourists can hardly believe their luck: the scene is picturesque—moose with full rack gazing over black waters, mountain walls and forest looming behind—and their cameras start snapping.

The moose strolls into the pond right up to his neck—head and rack seeming to float on water—and swims toward the tourists.

They become animated as it dawns on them that the moose is coming right at them. *Will it attack? Do moose bite?*

In a few minutes, the moose rises dripping out of the pond and stands before them.

The tourists shriek and toss peanut butter sandwiches and French fries at the beast's feet.

The moose is unflappable. It stands still for the photographers, feeds on the junk they have offered it, then, bored, turns and heads back toward the water.

In a few moments, the moose glides away from its thousandth interview with the ape.

With enough exposure and time, even the beasts of the field pick up the ape's venal habits.

Smithsonian Otters

The riverbank of the captive North American river otter *(Lontra canadensis)* is encapsulated in an aquarium, a sort of port hole for civilized apes to gape through to witness their alternate selves.

She moves in water with such sleek and graceful swiftness— appearing suddenly up on "shore" then disappearing right in front of the apes' eyes—that they swear there are several swimmers in the exhibit, though she is just one, driven by boredom to ever seek relief from her facsimile habitat.

Domestication strips adaptations of use.

Taking a Tumble

The pouter, the fantail, and the tumbler stood before the child, who was scouting out a subject for her school project.

The pouter left its perch, wafted around the coop, and returned to its roost to primp, seeming to strain on its toes for attention.

The fantail, too, took off on a display flight, and returned to show off its fine span of feathers.

The homely tumbler, like an ape on ice, launched into a spill,[69] and, cloaca over crop, plummeted to the ground—to be picked up by the girl, who had found herself a project.

To have culture is to delight in the improbable—the maladaptive, even.

A Primate's Wonderment

Two capuchin monkeys (*Cebus apella*) found themselves in the care of a great ape who would literally hand to them their every need, provided they agree to perform several absurd, tiresome tasks for the ape's amusement.[70]

When one of the monkeys indulged the ape's desire to have rocks given to it as favors, the ape rewarded it with slices of cucumber. Likewise for his mate in the next cage over: He, too, got cucumbers for his efforts. It was a sordid arrangement, but at least all were content.

Then the ape, inexplicably, began exchanging ripe grapes for the rocks the other monkey was procuring for the ape, even as our monkey continued to receive cucumbers.

So, our monkey picked up a rock, carefully burnished it on his fur, and held it out to the ape with a smile.

The ape took the rock and meted out cucumber.

The monkey flung the insipid morsel away, pummeled the walls of his enclosure, and spat at his ape ward, "After all my obedience, why use me thus?"

The ape moralized, "In this way we witness the need for fairness all primates deserve."

The monkey raged, "What sort of primate goes to such absurd lengths to see the obvious?"

Tadpoles

As a boy and his mother approached, the little pond quivered with movement just below the surface. The boy crouched and saw, in very shallow waters along the pond's scummy edge, a million black commas wriggling for attention.

"Look, Mom, fish!"

"No, honey, tadpoles. Those will turn into frogs."

"When, now?"

"In a few days."

Anticipating the flood of frogs soon to come, the boy returned to the pond a few days later with a friend to view the spectacle.

The two boys swarmed the edges of the pond and peered in, looking for tadpoles: there were none.

As for frogs: the boys looked, they scoured. Just once, near a stand of cattails, did the boys disturb a survivor,[71] which disappeared from their prying eyes with a discrete *ploop*.

Amphibian Tales

The biologist leafs through a textbook with his daughter, marveling at the rise of the four-legged animals, the tetrapods.[72] Through them, he tells her the tale of the history of error:[73]

"This is *Tiktaalik*.[74] If you were to ask *Tiktaalik*, 'Where did you come from?', he might say, 'Notice how we have eyes on the top of our heads. We are designed—doomed, perhaps—to always peep upward out of the water into the trees. It seems only obvious that we dropped out of those trees and will one day head back up there where we belong.'

"This next one is *Ichthyostega*,"[75] says Dad. "If you ask *Ichthyostega* whether he, too, dropped out of the trees, he might say, 'As we are always moving forward in our element, and as each day brings us to a new, watery place, I can only conclude that we create ourselves, for I cannot imagine living in a world of limited potential.'

"And now this one is *Anthracosaurus*.[76] Ask her, 'How did you get here? Is it through your own effort, or did you drop out of the trees?', she will say, 'Neither. A long time ago, our ancestors were mere fishes with bony fins for limbs. Over time, it became sensible for them to step out of the water—to chase flies, escape predators, whatever, it's no matter—and step they did, or those suited to it, anyway. With each step, they left the water behind and headed for the hills—and here we are.'"

"But how does *Anthracosaurus* know this?" the girl asks her father, the biologist.

"Well, as she puts it, 'I simply turned my head around and looked back the way I came!'"

"Alligator eats boy in nature preserve"

The image of those eyes popping up out of the surface of the algae-green lake was a hoot. The tourist just had to get a good shot of it.

"Honey, have Bobby stand close to the edge there so I can get him in the shot, too."

The last thing the parents saw was the boy's sneakers disappearing below the water's surface.

Later, an alligator was seen crossing the causeway to get to the other side. It never made it, however; it got run over by a tractor trailer.

Species command their domains.

A Kitten's Kittens

When the petite, black calico appeared in the leaf-strewn backyard—a swollen, gray tick attached above her left eye—the little girl became insufferable to her family.

"Look how small it is!" she urged. "If we don't do something before winter comes, it will die!"

Her mother agreed to assist in tracking down the little cat in the thicket that grew in the ditch behind the house.

"She's certainly too big now for her own mother to take care of," the girl's mother said.

At last, they found the little cat standing on a rock, looking alarmed.

As they approached it, the cat took off—and all her kittens scattered into the ditch to conceal themselves.

Life's cycles proceed apace.

Overturning Stones

It was the perfect spot for the children to build their fort—level, grassy, free of stones (except for one flat one). They could look down on the woods trail winding up the side of the ravine, and they would feel safe there.

They decided that after they had cleared the space, they would haul in sapling poles and cedar boughs to construct a magnificent shelter that would protect them from storms and conceal them from the losers in the neighborhood.

But first, this flat stone had to go. The larger boy hooked his fingernails on the edge of the rock and tried wriggling it free.

When this failed, he found a narrow stick with which to pry the rock up—the other two children leaning in close, urging him on—and the stone popped out of the earth.

As he kicked it over with his sneaker, some wormy things promptly withdrew into their dark holes; a few leggy arthropods scattered and ran; and—this was unmistakable—a little snake whipped off into tall grass.

The other boy and the girl shrieked in unison and fled back down the woods trail toward home—no, this was not a safe spot, after all—leaving the boy alone with his finds.

It is the nature of discovery to discompose.

Thus Spoke The Proterozoan

The fossil hunter had mortgaged his life to look for The Proterozoan,[77] the first animal. He abandoned his marriage and children, lost friends, and steeped himself in debt, just to travel around the world and break open slabs of black shale and examine them. For his efforts, he contracted a spirochete in India, a parasite in Canada, and a virus in China.

The search for The Proterozoan even infected his dreams: One night, in an antechamber of academe, surrounded by the gleanings of talus slopes and road cuts, the fossil hunter jimmied open a flake of Pre-Cambrian shale and at last uncovered the first stain of life, preserved there in the black rock.

"Finally!" he said. "What secrets do you have to transmit to us, a billion years hence?"

"Why plague us?" The Proterozoan asked. "We were enjoying our reprieve from the suffering."

143

Parable of the Unsinkable Optimist

In days gone by, a boatman took on board his bark ten travelers, in a passage on an estuary notorious for the ruin brought upon pilgrims.

During the voyage, one traveler clubbed another to death and picked his pocket. Thus, the boatman's trade was defamed with rumors of mayhem.

Sometime later, in old times, this boatman's descendant plied these same waters with a larger, sturdier vessel. He could take on board fifty travelers.

One night a spy slit three throats in an act of rebellion. Thus, this ferryman's trade was defamed like his ancestor's.

"Nay," said he. "Forty-seven travelers made it to the lee unmolested, whereas in days of yore only nine made it to safety."

Much later, in the more recent past, a newer seaman piloted an iron boat across the estuary. He commanded a crew of 100 and 450 passengers.

One evening two gangsters shot to death eight people in the ship's saloon when the lid was blown off a gambling scheme.

The reputation of the whole enterprise was endangered, until the pilot said, "In olden times, the death rate was 6%. It has now fallen to under 2%. Traveling is safer than ever."

Just recently a great ship, *The Optimist*, left the historic landing where the previous entrepreneurs plied their trade, laden with 1,600 passengers and crew.

Halfway to their destination, a madman armed with a .223 caliber semi-automatic weapon mowed down 20 innocent passengers on the decks, screaming, "Stop looking at me!"

The captain delightedly reported that the death rate had "fallen to an historical low of 1.25%."

The Fossil

Somebody's grandmother closed the book on a flower and forgot about it. When she died, her books went to the local library. When the library shut down, this book ended up on a table under a tent in the hot sun.

The new girl likes the green hard covers, the embossed print on the spine, the gilded pages. When she opens the book to an illustration, this illustration—the flower, now as fragile and translucent as a dragonfly's wing—almost slides off the page.

"Dad, it's somebody's violet!"

Using his yellowed nails as pincers, he plucks the flower off the text.

"No." Dad's a professor and extension agent. "Butterwort."

He deposits the flower back in its tomb. She is crestfallen.

"While it was alive," he says, "it ate tiny flies."

She stares with renewed interest at the page on which the flower reposes.

"Yes"—he speaks right into her silence—"that flower was carnivorous."

Where have they all gone, those flies? This flower could not have finished digesting them all when it died. She imagines chewed-up arthropods' body parts stacked among dead cell walls, whole lives embedded in tissue that outstrips time itself.

Observant Ape

On his way home, a hominin saw two corvids feeding on sciurid roadkill, flat as a flounder. The birds up and flew away when they noticed the hominin's truck bearing down on them.

He wondered about the intersection of human and animal: on the one hand, because of human meddling, a sciurid dies a faultless death; on the other, some corvids enjoy a feast.

He concluded that the reign of the apes is a disaster that yet presents many opportunities. It is not like there is a direction or goal to any of it, though. Evolution may even see it fit that the apes drive themselves collectively into a ditch in the meantime.

Had the sciurid wings, it would have lofted out of the path of the vehicle that killed it, like those corvids.

Were they still flightless reptiles, the corvids would be roadkill.

And had an asteroid not struck the planet 66 million years ago—

PART THREE

Tales from Flyspeck Farm

CHAPTER SEVEN

Barnyard Fables

The Sky Pest

Some turkeys (*Meleagris gallopavo*) had become closely associated with the flat-faced, long-legged ape over many generations. It is doubtful whether these birds were cognizant of their dependency on this ape or whether they could even see the wire fence in front of their beaks. But they were bright enough to know when the fretful farmer was about to toss some stale buns over the fence—and so was the crow (*Corvus brachyrhynchus*).

Like a bolt of the blackest lightning, the crow sailed from oak top, to maple crown, to elm limb and thence to the ground, and was already flapping off with a whole bun in its beak before the farmer could wave, "Shoo! Shoo!", leaving the turkeys in the middle of a crazed dance of confusion and alarm.

Domestication yields mutual opportunism.

The Rooster's Lot

The barn owl (*Tyto alba*) was an efficient killer, swift and deadly; but it did not lack grace and tact as did the fowl (*Gallus*). Flying in a morning provision of vole for his wife, the owl returned to the cavity high in a pine tree for his daily rest. There they hunkered down over their eggs to watch the antics in the barnyard below.

The fretful farmer kept a few roosters along with his hens in a shed and yard, a rectangle of dust and droppings surrounded by flimsy wire. The main cock crowed at about the time the owl was thinking of retiring. It was often said that the rooster's crow signaled the owl to bed—a canard that the owl found particularly galling.

In the morning, the rooster wasted no time setting about the task of keeping the members of his harem in line and humiliating the young cockerel that had been permitted to live alongside the flock.[78]

Everything about this animal bespoke violence: the provocative scarlet comb erupting from its head; the strutting gait accompanied by a set of daunting spurs; the obscene speech preceded by the clamorous flapping of useless wings. The cock was simultaneously corn-fed and arrogant, a despicable disposition.

But these mannerisms were as nothing compared to his appalling behavior. He sidled up to and mounted hens at his pleasure, using his beak to grab onto combs and stabilize himself on their submissive backs.

If the young cockerel so much as took note of this, the cock flew at him with spurs raised and dashed him to the dirt. Naturally, the young rooster had some fight in him and would attempt to defend himself; but his master was larger, better equipped, and more experienced.

The old rooster had learned to press the young one into a corner of the yard and pin it against the wire. Then he would set about tearing out the new tail feathers growing out the young backside and scarring up the comb that grew above bright eyes.

The racket put up by the disarmed cockerel was awful. The cock would release him only for short intervals to cringe—disheveled and bloodied—in a new corner of the yard.

This is how the cock spent its days in service of the harem—until one day the farmer dispatched him.

Disgusted, the owls turned their broad faces away and huddled in their modest cavity. Exhausted from the hunt, they shut their eyes against the din and settled in upon quiescent eggs.

Contemplating our neighbor's lot helps us appreciate our own humble station.

The Ritual Layer

The Araucana hen found a gap in the wire fence that enclosed the fretful farmer's chicken yard. She escaped and disappeared under the board pile to lay her egg; when she emerged again, she was distressed to realize she could not get back in with her flock mates, and she paced back and forth along the base of the wire fencing, clucking.

The farmer, thinking she had flown over the top of the fence, grabbed her against the wire and tossed her back in over the top, saying, "Dumb cluck." It was his opinion that pullets were "stupid as shit," and good only as long as they laid eggs.

The next afternoon after collecting eggs, the farmer opened the hen house door—and the Araucana bolted past the other exiting hens and made for the hole in the wire. Before the farmer could catch her, she disappeared under the board pile to lay an egg. The farmer was miffed, but now he knew her secret; and so, after tossing the hen back over the top again, he closed the gap in the fence by twisting the strands of wire upon one another.

Now, every afternoon when released from the house, the Araucana races to the fence around the yard and paces back and forth in front of the spot where the gap used to be, and she never gives up her search.

Even nostalgia has its lowly origins.[79]

151

Foraging

After pouring a bucket of grain into the feeder, the fretful farmer picked up an inert Speckled Sussex from the hen house floor. Its tail feathers were gone, and its scab-encrusted rump was already putrescent. The farmer glanced over at the other hens arranged along their wooden perch, all giving him their left eye.

"You would pick off the prettiest one amongst you," he said.

A Rhode Island Red rejoined, "You expect us to stop foraging, just because you've clamped us into this isolation?"

Adaptive traits, thwarted, become pathologies.

Chicken

Led in by the scent of grain, the tiny *Mus musculus* found itself in the chicken coop, where it was immediately set upon by hens.

The mouse took off, but an ever-vigilant Leghorn seized it with her beak and repeatedly dashed it against the floorboards, stunning it.

The mouse now in a catatonic state, the hen snatched it up by the tail and began to scurry about the house with it dangling, looking for a place to enjoy her meat all to herself—but there was no place to go!

The other hens, now jealous of her find, chased after her, trying to snatch the prize from her beak.

She ended up running around in circles, with a windfall she could not enjoy.

The mere possession of a resource depletes it.

Corvid vs. Farmer

The fretful farmer did not realize that the crow was stalking him from the trees. The bird's cries of "Hah! Hah!" to its cohorts blended in with the background mayhem of nature. It was his absence that was being monitored. So, when the farmer hoisted the flat of fruit and left the strawberry bed, the crow occupied it.

To flush the corvid out, the farmer had to put the tray down and return to the bed to clap his hands, whereupon the crow took off, swooped down, and plucked a strawberry off the top of the unattended flat with his beak in mid-flight.

Grace is the hallmark of the adapted.

Guts

Flustered by the wire mesh of her enclosure, pacing near the spot where she knew an escape hole should be, the Araucana hen found she could loft herself the full height of the fence. She made it over the top on her final attempt, unbeknownst to the fretful farmer. She was thus free to return to her clutch of eggs under the board pile and brood there as in old days.

As he was securing the hen house that evening, the farmer did not realize there was one less bird inside. But a good whiff of the interior told him the house would need cleaning.

The next day, the farmer discovered a small pile of gray fluff and covert feathers lying in the dirt beside a complete intestinal tract. There was nothing else, no body parts, no blood, just downy feathers and glossy guts left behind by a tidy predator. The farmer wondered who it could be—who the mammal, who the bird.

Absently, he unlatched the gate and swung it open to permit the chickens to run while he got ready to shovel out the house.

Several hens immediately scrambled over to their comrade's guts and wolfed them down.

Indiscriminate feeding at least assures priority.

The Stoat's Reasoning

The hens in the keep of the fretful farmer found themselves at the mercy of an ermine (*Mustela*) in the small hours. The winds having blown decayed shingles off the henhouse, this stoat was able to gain access between chinks in the boards.

His small stature was no handicap when it came to worrying the large birds: he caused an appalling disturbance in the house, and soon all the hens were flying against the boards and raising dust.

The ermine mounted the back of one hen and bit her spine in half. He then severed the head and began feasting on blood. Soon, to the outrage of the other hens, he was looking around for another kill, gripping a young pullet and bringing her down. Then he sought another ...

"You have killed enough to feed your entire family!" a hen admonished the stoat. "Why not spare the rest of us?"[80]

The beast's red mouth fell open, incredulous.

"What, and leave you all to the mercy of my nemesis, the sneaky raccoon?"

Killing fulfills strategic needs as well as appetites.

Rattled

The timber rattler (*Crotalus horridus*) hated being hated. No one ever considered that this snake sensed hostility and that the continual rejection scarred her psyche. She had never harmed any creature that was not a food source for her. She vowed to be more unobtrusive and to just go about her business with care and caution.

She slithered into a lumber pile and curled up between boards to sleep where no one could find her. She hunted out behind the pile only when she had to, eating mice and voles and rats: very frugal and particular about her diet, she was. She could even be considered a remover of pest species. She spent most of the day curled between the cool pine boards, remote from bother, content to slumber.

There was a rumbling, sliding sound, then a *clap*. This repeated itself many times, this sliding and clapping. The fretful farmer was removing boards from the pile and tossing them aside, looking for the right width board to work with. Suddenly the snake was exposed: instinctively, looking up at the light, she shook her rattle in alarm.

A few whacks with a pine board did her in.[81]

When one's mere presence is an affront to others, nothing will prevent calumny from being heaped upon one's head.

Portrait of a Bovid

The cow (*Bos*) has no detectable emotions. Mostly static, unperturbed, she spends her time sitting on her duff, ruminating. There are no secrets. *I am hungry. I am pregnant. I am tired.* Boredom is not in her repertoire: There is no appetite for novelty in her to cause her to be bored by anything whatsoever.

She will sometimes walk like she is on a mission, pacing up the hill like she has somewhere to go. She, amazingly, seems to have no idea that while she is walking she is defecating. With fouled legs, she goes and stands under a tree. It is not even raining, or sunny.

Flies: flies do seem to inspire her, and you had better be careful when she suddenly gets the urge to swing her rack of horns around to slap a long strand of slobber against her fly-encrusted flank. When she has to enter the barn to get out of the flies, you get out of the way.

Once, a young bull was presented to her—it was time, cows have a very brief window of opportunity to breed—and when the bull got the lip-curl the cow lowered her horns and went after him. She was having none of it.[82]

Sometimes, reclining, her legs folded underneath her as daintily as a cat's, you almost sense how the ancients conceived their gods.

158

Pigs at the Trough

The pigs (*Sus*) were jostling each other and squalling before the milk and apples even made it into the trough. The larger of the two threw its excess weight around, blocking the other's access to the food, while the more petite one took advantage of its relative unobtrusiveness to worm its snout between the larger one's hooves and suck some milk from the trough. Discovering this outrage, the larger one shrieked and rooted its mate's jowls out of the trough.

They had been fed regularly for months, the farmer never failing to arrive at the specified morning and evening feeding times.

If he made any noise upon entering the barn, the pigs grunted and tumbled about, nipping at each other in anticipation, even hopping up on the wooden sides of their stall and barking for attention. The slop was always delightful: surplus cow's milk; apple culls; expired cartons of donuts and loaves of bread; damaged or too-small sweet potatoes and squash; plus a #10 can of commercial swine pellets thrown in for good measure.

But the more abundantly the pigs were fed, the greedier they became.

The bigger one continued to outgrow the small one, the runt squealing about the other's hooves, yet managing to eek enough of a meal to bring it to a satisfactory market weight.

"They're well-fed, all right," the farmer remarked to the butcher, "but you would never know it listening to them complain all winter."

Gluttony is the innate apprehension of scarcity.

Pork

Two winter pigs found their pen door had been left open, so they pushed through into the side run of the barn, delightedly frolicking in the shavings-strewn space.

Further investigation led the pair to a ramp that connected to an adjacent chamber, a cozy little box containing a thick bed of hay, some broken pumpkins, and a bucket of grain.

They barged into this tight area, sniffed it out, then turned and hightailed it out of there: this was but a test; there was no harm.

They returned and settled in, for the hay was fragrant and the grain sweet. There they lay, side-by-side, until the fretful farmer closed the trailer gate and latched it.

The gentlest of deceptions can be the most devastating.

Rams

Cumulus—so named because his fleece was a roiling thundercloud of color—was a fecund, placid daddy (if such may be said of an ovid). His nemesis was another ram named Hammer, white as cotton batting, pugnacious and unyielding, a gay warrior. Again, such a designation may be in error; but ewes did not interest him.[83]

Cumulus stepped aside politely whenever the other ram tried to engage him. "Nice try, my friend."

As the lambs of Cumulus, like scuds of cloud, rambled over the hillsides feeding, Hammer, in frustration, stove apart the barn stall with his forehead.

It got so the fretful farmer could not enter the pen without a length of two-by-four in-hand.

He eventually got around to storing Hammer in the freezer. This was nothing personal, mind you.

Raising the products of evolution to serve our interests is a decidedly illiberal activity.

161

Twice-Crazy Horse

The fretful farmer led his horse, a high-strung, old Standardbred, from the barn to a waiting horse trailer, to be transported to summer pastures.

While walking through the barnyard, they passed a garbage can standing off to their left: the horse balked.

"This is surely a carnivore!" it shrieked, immediately adopting the stiff-legged, sprawling stance of a Windsor chair, rolling its eyes, and snorting like a beast.

The farmer kept a firm hold on the horse's halter to prevent it from bolting. He had to return the horse to the barn, remove the predatory trash receptacle, then reapproach the trailer with the horse, while reassuring it that everything was OK.

In the autumn, the horse was returned to the farm and unloaded from the trailer; whereupon being led by the farmer, the horse saw the garbage can standing this time off to the right. The horse reared at the end of its lead line and yanked the farmer back toward the trailer.

The farmer muckled two-handedly onto the horse's halter, brought it under control and spoke into its face:

"We have been through this before, now settle down!"

"You should know better!" the panicked horse admonished the fretful farmer. "I have two brains,[84] and that makes me twice as crazy!"

Our disposition depends entirely on how we are put together.

The Feral Felid

The feral felid hangs around the barn and approaches the house, hoping to find a tidbit left behind by the fretful farmer or one of his house cats.

The youngest tabby cat crouches on the windowsill behind the screen and pines for life out of doors. Sensing the feral cat in the shadows, it growls from the safety of its screen. But the screen is in sad shape and falls out of the window.

The house cat leaps after the intruder and starts a ruckus: there is much hooting and hollering as the two size each other up.

"I am master of the barn," says the feral one. "Uncollared, I come and go as I please. Bats, toads and voles are my fare. No cold tinned foods or window screens for me!"

The house cat creeps nearer and bats a paw at the feral one. "Indeed. As I am fat, you are lean. While I snooze the night away, you hunt. I envy the life you lead."

A tussle ensues, and the house cat takes note: The feral one is nasty, with notches taken out of its ears; coarse, burr-napped fur; and a deformed claw. In addition to a belly bloated with nematodes, it has fleas, ticks, and bad teeth. It is scrappy, though—"I defend with my life my right to inhabit this barn"—and the house cat backs off.

"Have at it," says the tabby, leaping back through the open window.

Better contemplate the authentic lifestyle than live it.

Canids

The fretful farmer wakes at a bleak, chill 3 a.m., thinking he is hearing children screaming on a carnival ride. High-pitched wails punctuate the night silence—coyotes! And so close to the house. He begins counting cats in his head and drifts off . . .

Life for coyotes (*Canis*) is all about pacing. They have to outpace the rugged lynx and the wolf to catch the hopping lagomorphs that they like to feed to their pups. They are continually having to outpace fleas and ticks, parasites and mange, diseases like rabies that have brought down many in the family—to say nothing of the guns of the flat-faced ape. On it goes throughout their range, the chasing and the fleeing.

A monogamous pair might pursue an ungulate into deep snow, surround her and her fawn, then leap on their necks. There would be food enough to carry, piece-by-piece, back to their den of pups. But in this appallingly hard year, they must approach the hominins' habitat: Has the fretful farmer remembered to shut the chicken house door? Are there any newborn calves about? How vigilant has he been about keeping his felids indoors?

A plump, marbled tabby cat walks the stone wall that separates the apes' range from the wild, its coat reflecting late winter moonlight.[85]

When the coyotes leap, the cat's shrieks disappear in the yipping of celebrating canids.

Negligence serves as handmaiden to predation.

The Heritage Tom

Some heritage turkeys were overwintered by the fretful farmer to bolster the supply of spring poults to raise for next year's meat.

In April, as the hens sat mesmerized inside a shed on their clutch of eggs, the tom engaged in perpetual displays in the yard, inflating himself at nothing, puffing and humming without provocation. But provocation was what he sought, and the least response drew him on.

His coarse, stammering chuckling was endless; his caruncles grew as livid as a bunch of blood-filled grapes; and his primary feathers scraped dirt as he modeled and turned.

He sidled up to the fretful farmer once, enraged by the ape's presumption of existence, and leaped at him.

The tom got the fight he wanted—and lost his head—but at least his eggs were safe.[86]

Natural selection concerns itself not in the least with our persons.

A Curiosity

The shy but scrappy felid was led to occupy the fretful farmer's barn for the occasional rodent and reprieve from the cold.

There were endless opportunities for privacy and shelter amongst the piles of old farm equipment, under stacks of boards, and in empty animal stalls. He was soon familiar with the entire geography of the old building, which became his preferred haunt, though he had to share it with the pointy-faced 'possum that foraged the barn for orphaned hens' eggs.

When the farmer mentioned to his veterinarian that an opossum had moved into his barn and had taken to meddling with the trash bags and pilfering grain from bins, the veterinarian explained that the opossum may harbor a protozoan[87] that could infect the crazy old Standardbred the farmer had inherited from his grandfather.

The veterinarian suggested the farmer trap the animal and release it elsewhere. But the farmer decided that not only would this be a pain in the you-know-what, he did not want to just pawn the problem off on somebody else.

So, he set leghold traps baited with fatty food scraps to rid the barn of the intruder.

Any new feature or disturbance in the felid's domain always drew the curious felid on, and fatty food was irresistible.

His unhappy fate, simply a case of mistaken identity, illustrated to the fretful farmer's chagrin that the simple presence of temptation suggests a will somewhat less than free.

That Sneaky Raccoon

Turkey poults were expensive to purchase; so, to make sure he was not just feeding the wildlife with them, the fretful farmer built a woven-wire turkey house up on two-by-four stilts to keep them above the reaches of the vicious stoat, the lone coyote, and the flamboyant skunk.

The young turkeys had a dry roof to roost under, a protected feed box, and a slatted floor that allowed their droppings to fall out of the way to the ground. The farmer refilled their waterer through a plank door held shut by a turn button. Little did the farmer know what a dexterous creature *Procyon lotor* is.

One night while the farmer was away, the raccoon climbed up on the door, turned the button with his little hands, and let himself in.

When the fretful farmer returned, he found the door wide open and bloodied turkey carcasses on the slatted floor, on the ground outside the house, even on the roof of the house. The beast had killed them all.[88]

"Serves me right for not anticipating the raccoon." The farmer added a catch to the plank door, an iron staple hasp held shut with a horse lead line clip. That would foil that sneaky raccoon. The farmer repopulated the poultry house.

A few nights later, the raccoon took himself under the turkey house, stood up, reached his little hands up through the slatted floor, and pulled the legs right off the young birds.

Adaptations may be employed in ways that exceed their original uses.

The Cat's Atrocity

The fretful farmer pauses in his summer pruning to watch his felid companion torment a vole (*Microtus*). It is the reason he keeps the orchard grass mowed so short: to expose the voles so the cat can find them—voles eat the bark on young trees, which kills them—but now he almost can't bear the cat's behavior.

This felid has spent half an hour batting the live vole around, letting it jump and perform terror antics in the grass, then taking it in its mouth by the head and carrying it to the farmer.

The felid now lounges in the grass near the stone wall, looking on placidly, while the vole threads an escape route through the grass blades. When the vole gets too far away, the felid springs from its lounge and pounces, snatching the vole up in its jaws and bringing it back, dumping it in the grass.

The vole pants rapidly, its tick-like eyes black with despair.

The farmer is indignant: "What if I aimed my rifle at your head, repeatedly cocked it, and pulled the trigger on an empty chamber, just to torment you?"

"You wouldn't do that to me," says the felid. "Those are the torments you reserve for your own kind."

The Flicker

During the tedium of morning barn chores, the fretful farmer heard the dreaded *rat-a-tat tat* of a creature beating itself to death against the highest window at the barn's gable end.

Despite his being responsible for the deaths of animals in the thousands, the tapping sound immediately broke the farmer's heart, for it was the sound of the futility of creatures trapped in an ape's world.

He looked up and saw a relentless black fluttering against the bottom center pane of the lower window sash. The bird was desperate to get out, and it knew which way to go—that way, toward where the trees lay—and expended its dearest effort to reach them, even hammering against the glass.

It took some time, but the fretful farmer got out his extension ladder and hauled the rungs up via the rope lanyard to the limits of the ladder's length. He carefully propped the ladder rails against a horizontal beam, just below the window, and climbed up.

There, bunched against its invisible but implacable barrier, befouled with tangles of cobwebs, was the bird, a flicker (*Colaptes auratus*), with marvelous black spots on its tummy!

He cupped the bird against the glass with his hands, shifted it to one hand, and descended the ladder using his free hand.

At the bottom, he had barely opened his palm to help clear the bird of webs when the flicker flashed yellow toward the treetops.

Instinct once activated is curtailed only by culture.

Home to Roost

The dilapidated chicken coop having finally become a hazard to its occupants, the fretful farmer decided one night to transfer the slumbering birds to new quarters in the barn, there to remain through the upcoming winter. He dismantled the flimsy fencing and razed the old building, leaving behind just the dingy rectangle of bare dirt where for years the chickens had scratched.

In the barn, the crazy old Standardbred, always exquisitely attuned to minute shifts in his environment, noticed that the top half of the double-hung door adjoining his stall, which heretofore had always remained open, was now closed; so, he instructed his nervous lips to work the latch until it swung free.

Now liberated, the hens scattered to all corners of the barn and property, laying eggs in feeding troughs, on hay bales, and under board piles, while the horse occupied himself for the afternoon at the chickens' grain dispenser.

A wary Leghorn confided to the matronly Barred Rock: "We endanger our necks by scattering ourselves and our eggs thus around the property!"

"Don't worry," the Rock responded. "By nightfall, we will all be gathered back on our perch as we usually are, and the farmer will have already forgiven us."

That evening, the Barred Rock said, "Follow me," and led the entire flock back down to the dirt square where their old digs used to be. They squatted there in the dark, until a lone canid showed up.

Ingrained habits and blind obeisance subvert our most fervent intentions.

I, Dinosaur

Plumed for conquest, the Bourbon Red turkey strutted and turned and chuckled in the barnyard, striving to be the plum in the eye of a hen attending skeptically nearby.

All was going well for the tom—until the neighbor's little spaniel downwind caught whiff of the ripe feast and took off across the road to interrupt the ceremonial dance.

In an instant, the puffed-up bird deflated and assumed the waddling, ancestral gait of his lizard forebears, fleeing the scene, fantail folded to a stem. No time to think, just run.

The canid loped along with its tongue out of its mouth, seeming to smile as it closed the gap between itself and the bird.

The turkey darted and dodged; the dog chomped its tail.

With a screechy whistle, the bird launched upward toward a tree branch, relinquishing its tail feathers[89] along the way as readily as a child releasing a fistful of dandelion fuzz.

The dog shook the trash out of its jaws and snap-barked at the bird. The bird stood tailless in the tree, nothing left for it to do but stare down at its usurper.

Ornamentation proclaims the expendable nature of beauty.

The Ducks and their Drake

Newly released from their night quarters by the fretful farmer, the drake and attendant ducks (*Anas platyrhynchos*) race down toward the pond, waddling in ceremonious single file, the drake hissing admonitions and the ducks quacking in supplication.

Once upon the water the drake visits each of his acolytes in turn and forcibly copulates with her, pinching the back of her head with his tough beak, hopping on her back and submersing her beneath the waves.

The duck does not readily submit but does what any ravished communicant does—put up a struggle at first, as if not knowing what was to come.

We are at the mercy of what we believe in.

The Haunting

The fretful farmer recognized the signs: cats pawing and scratching at walls until wallpaper tore; box-stored apples in the cellar shredded; horse droppings broken apart and hauled throughout the barn into wall cavities, between hay bales, underneath feeding troughs. One night he even caught a flicker of movement in the pig pen in the penumbra of his flashlight.

And so, a fruitless pursuit began, commencing with rugged snap traps baited with sunflower seeds, then cheese, then scraps of bacon. The farmer graduated to specially built buckets filled with liquid antifreeze and rigged with a coffee can slathered in peanut butter that rotated horizontally on a wire, the bucket fitted with a plank ramp up to the rim for his victims' convenience. The rats—content with their horseshit and apples—ignored the farmer's tricks and devices.

As weeks passed with no bodies showing up, and stored produce continuing to diminish, and smelly piles of rat turds on the increase, the farmer bought poison hotels from the hardware store and placed them strategically around the barn, which hotels the rats refused to check into.

Overhead in the house now, there was scuffling and scratching that drove the cats to such distraction they launched themselves off furniture to claw at the moldings.

The farmer took the poison blocks out of their hotels and placed them directly into holes, cavities, raceways around the barn, but with discretion, fretting all the while about his cats and turkeys and chickens. He could only wait now.

In a final gesture of contempt, the rats opted to die trapped between the floor and ceiling above the fretful farmer's bedroom, plaguing him long after their deaths.

CHAPTER EIGHT

Parables of Rural Life

The Apple Grove

The neighbor who bought the land next to Flyspeck Farm had a little orchard in her backyard. This new owner was deeply concerned about Mother Nature. Her concern extended to "pollinators," "non-target species," and "human beings." She was determined in her care of the apple grove to allow Nature to take its course, for with Nature all turns out right in the end.

In the spring, she did not spray fungicides because someone did a study that showed an association between fungicides and some cancerous cells and she did not want to take that risk.

She did not spray insecticides, either, for similar health reasons, and because she didn't want to disrupt the local ecology. "Sprays kill everything that has a right to live on this planet," she told her neighbor, the fretful farmer. "Think of the bees."

Fungi and arthropods of all stripes expressed their gratitude by occupying all the niches she had secured for them.

In the summer, she allowed the grasses and broad-leafed plants to grow tall among the trunks to provide a meadow between the rows of trees. She did not use weed killers because she heard they were toxic. Besides, natural undergrowth creates a habitat for local beneficial species. "There is a natural balance that needs to be maintained for ecological health."

So, vining plants, voles and trunk borers took up residence amongst the trees.

In the fall, the nature lover held a harvest bash and invited over friends and neighbors, including the fretful farmer, to help pick the remaining apples and press them into cider.

Knowing how nature does not reckon our fine intentions, the farmer was not at all surprised to find a lot of small, scabby, insect-damaged fruit.

Part-time Herbivore

The new neighbor wished to be known as a vegetarian who nonetheless could not abide the dogmatism of veganism.

She saw no harm, for example, in harvesting honey from the beehive; for surely the bee would be delighted to know that we appreciated her labors.

Milk and cheese products were permitted, only if they came from organic cows allowed to graze fresh pastures.

While she preferred an omelet made with the unfertilized eggs of free-range pullets, she was satisfied with the eggs the fretful farmer sold.

But she would not outright "eat anything with a central nervous system."

One day as she was buying eggs from the farmer, he inquired into the origins of her leather handbag, whether such cows had access to green grass.

The nature lover, proud of her accessory, declared, "It's goatskin. My husband got it for me before he died."

The Screaming Marmot

The fretful farmer's new neighbor, a lover of nature, enjoyed her spring bulbs—or would have, had the marmot not enjoyed them more.

These were naturalized bulbs that came with the estate—crocus, hyacinth, and jonquil, even long-lived tulips. The old woman who lived there before had left a colorful legacy on the bank of the ditch in front of the house. The new neighbor weeded and thinned and mowed to keep the bulbs safe from encroachment and was delighted when their green shoots showed up in early spring—even in snow!

The tulips were the last to bloom. As the expired crocuses declined to pitiful-looking strings, the tulips put up robust buds amid stout leaves—and the marmot had her eye on them.

One morning the neighbor parted her curtains to check on the progress of the tulips and saw a furry brown rump busily chewing, chewing. The creature snuck up to a swollen tulip bud—its green outer petals just starting to take on the red-stained look at the seams—bent it down with one, deft sweep of its claw and bit it off the stem. Behind the marmot stood a jagged line of decapitated tulips' stems.

The woman leaped out her door and screamed, "Git!", then looked around sharply to see if her neighbor had seen.

This continued, day after day, until her tulips were nearly depleted of fresh buds. It did not matter that she had borrowed the fretful farmer's cage trap to dispose of the woodchuck properly; the marmot just turned up her nose at the apple and kale baits and went right for the pile of tulips.

One morning, just after twilight, the woman got up early to preempt the marmot. As she was sneaking around the corner of her house, toting the baited cage trap, she surprised the marmot barreling toward her from the other direction.

Caught between the foundation stone of the house and the big granite doorstep, the marmot flung its rump around and bunched up in the corner, startling the poor woman; and when she dropped the cage trap, the two mammals shrieked in each other's faces.

Instinct

The old cow had calved in a corner of the pasture, under a pine tree, as far away as the electric wire permitted, where she could not be seen.

The stillborn bull calf lay in the grass, inert as a hemlock log, the same mahogany color.

The cow continued to lick the dead calf's backside and chuckle to it.

The fretful farmer had a dilemma on his hands—how to get the cow back to the barn, for she was not about to leave the calf's side, and she could barely be led by her collar as it was.

The farmer grabbed the dead calf's hooves—one front one, one rear one—and began to drag it through the grass, walking backwards toward the barn.

Its long neck lolled pitifully, and a striking pink tongue stuck out between perfect front teeth. The whole well-formed animal was too beautiful not to be alive, and it sickened the farmer to drag it across the field like that.

But steadily, methodically he went, drawing along its chuckling mother, stopping periodically to allow her to catch up and lick her dead son.

In this way, he got the cow all the way back to the barn.

Robins

On the lawn below the window of the new neighbor, about a dozen robins (*Turdus migratorius*) scamper, pause: stare for a moment.

They seem oblivious to one another, pursuing their separate invertebrates in the sod.

Scamper, pause: stare for a moment.

The neighbor does not notice; they are about as interesting to her as dandelions in the grass or squirrels on the bird feeder.

She is too busy with her binoculars, scanning the trees over the heads of the robins. She is waiting for an erratic vagrant to show up, a big owl, perhaps, or a heron, or even the pileated woodpecker.

The robins, in busy pursuit of the invertebrates beneath her view, are colored turd-over-brick. They scamper, they pause: they stare for a moment.

They go *churp, cheep! chirrup.* Their toes look like worms.

Scamper, pause:

Remarkably, and for no good reason, they all leave the ground at once and take to the trees, like autumn foliage falling in reverse.

Hen

The fretful farmer's flock of layers includes one Araucana hen that will not shut up. She manages to stay quiet and blend in with the rest of the birds whenever the farmer is nearby. But when she is on her own—that is, when she is with just her own kind—oh, does she moan! It is a hoarse, drawn-out, cackle-moan, as if she were in perpetual mourning over something.

The effect puts the new neighbor, the lover of nature, on edge: "Can't you do something about that clucking chicken? She won't shut up."

The farmer watches carefully for a few days and discovers who the moaner is. Then he grasps the Araucana by the head and turns her neck like a crank.

"That's not what I meant!" laments the neighbor.

Demise of the Wily Pheasants

The fretful farmer's negligence was on display in his asparagus bed, which by late summer had become a nearly impenetrable wall of unfurled asparagus ferns and weeds.

One day the reclusive neighbor, who lived on property abutting Flyspeck Farm, saw a flock of pheasants in the farmer's backyard.

He got out his shotgun and opened his back door to shoot them, but the wily pheasants instinctively scrambled to conceal themselves within the dark verdure of the asparagus bed.

The neighbor simply whistled for his little spaniel and sat on his back porch with his gun across his knees.

Whenever the dog flushed a pheasant out of the asparagus, the neighbor stood and fired.

Wild Garden

In the spring the new neighbor would express her love of nature by refurbishing the perennial beds left to go feral after the previous owner of the house, a woman known for her prolific gardens and tasty preserves, a distant relative of the fretful farmer next door, was struck down by a cancer and rendered bedridden for several years until she died. In that time, the old lady's wildflower nook went into full retreat, her tidy humps of ornamentals and herbs expanded into thickets indistinguishable from one another, aggressive species of weeds pervading it all like the creeping mycelia of some horrible fungus. With weeding claw and root digger clenched in hands gloved for combat, the new neighbor attacked this mess—spearing, and carving, and shearing—until she had exposed to light the fundamental principle of horticulture: *Nature does not care.* Stolons of Solomon's seal (*Polygonatum*) were heavily involved with competing mats of horse mint (*Monarda*) and tansy (*Tanacetum*), precious bloodroot (*Sanguinaria*) roots languished under a carpet of *Iris,* wild Mayapple (*Podophyllum*) poking up here and there, the whole mess shot through with the rhizomes of quackgrass (*Elymus*), *Vinca*, and lily-of-the-valley (*Convallaria*). This chaos could not be rooted out. She had a vision of a painting seen in a college course, garish and disturbing—a Breughel? a Rubens?—of fighters' legs entwined in bitter brawling, of arms locked around heads, faces wild and contorted, fingers dug into biting mouths and clenched eyes, while women gathered around and danced a ritual dance of impotent intervention.

Skunked

In the skunk's estimation, there is nothing sweeter than the garbage can which the fretful farmer leaves beside the barn.

Inside this receptacle lies a sack of turkeys' heads and turkeys' feet and bloody turkey guts, which the farmer planned to take to the dump tomorrow, but tomorrow came and went.

He has thus insured that his neighbor's little spaniel, a sneaky raccoon, and even some of his own livestock get a good spraying from the skunk.

It is an eventful night, during which the skunk wages a flamboyant chemical campaign over the leftover bird parts, ruining everyone's appetite in the process.

Before the farmer shoots him, the skunk hisses, in effect: "If I can't have it, nobody can!"

Fair Weather Geese

The reclusive neighbor on the property adjacent to Flyspeck Farm kept geese because they were "good guard dogs."

No one came onto his land without being announced by cries and honks.

This worked well until their first winter, when the geese migrated over to the fretful farmer's place to live on top of the steaming shit pile beside his barn.

The neighbor could not entice the geese back onto his property.

They just honked in protest: "We still love you, but we love warm feet better."

Dead Sheep

The lover of nature had a shed built in her backyard, and she strung an electric wire around her little orchard, to raise a few sheep for herself.

She would shear, card, and spin her own wool, and knit old-timey Christmas presents for her nieces and nephews.

She bought a pregnant Romney ewe, which had a stillbirth.

So, she bought a few lambs from her neighbor, the fretful farmer, but one immediately got disemboweled by a pack of coyotes, and another managed to slip under the electric wire and get mangled by another neighbor's monster truck.

One just up and died, probably from eating sheep laurel ("lambkill") in her little pasture.

She bought more lambs and had her ewe bred again. Her hobby was becoming quite the investment.

She vented her frustrations to the fretful farmer, who listened patiently to her tales of woe.

"Dead sheep are becoming my specialty! What am I doing wrong?"

"Probably nothing," the farmer said. "A sheep is born trying to die."

The Porcupine Tree

While the fretful farmer was talking sheep with his idealistic neighbor in the late afternoon, they noticed two black lumps moving through the just-mowed hayfield—mama porcupine and her young one. The farmer hated this sight: He knew it would culminate in the porcupines' deaths.

"They're on the move. I wish they'd stay in the woods."

"They're adorable," the neighbor said.

"We'll see what you think once they start gnawing on your trees."

Over the next few days, he spied the baby porcupine in the open ground of the orchard in daylight. He went after it with his .22 pistol, but the farmer was not a very good shot and the baby waddled away. The porcupine disappeared under the board pile.

Another day a baby, perhaps the same one, was seen climbing the trunk of a maple tree, looking just like a Japanese beetle on an ear of corn. The fretful farmer raised his shotgun and fired, knocking the porcupine out of the tree and shooting a limb off in the process.

Mama porcupine was harder to track down. She was smarter, shier, and did her work on the apple trees after midnight. She dodged the farmer's traps and snares, kept an irregular schedule, moving from tree-to-tree, but usually favoring the Tollman Sweeting because its apples were sugary even when green

After two weeks of playing tag, and broken twigs, and chewed-off limbs, and small, green Tollmans all over the ground, the farmer finally caught up with her at one a.m. in a nearly denuded tree on the neighbor's property. He almost did not see her in the flashlight's beam—she was as still and silent as an apple herself—but a reflection in her pinhole eye gave her away. The discharge from the farmer's pistol pierced the August night air. The porcupine fell from the tree with a thump. He would deal with her after sunrise.

He and his neighbor took a tractor out to her tree after chore time. He got off and put on his heavy work gloves and gripped the porcupine by the tail—near the tip where it was not so spiny—and lifted her from the grass. She was hefty.

As she hung there above the tractor bucket, the neighbor gasped: The porcupine still had a little green apple gripped between her two claws.

Wrong Address

In her mailbox the lover of nature did not find the expected solicitations from wildlife funds nor any copies of nature magazines. Instead, she pulled out a firearms magazine and an apocalyptic flyer from a far-right organization, both addressed to her reclusive neighbor, whose field of FOR SALE signs abutted Flyspeck Farm.

She carried the mail down the road to the entrance of the neighbor's property and peered up his rutted driveway. She thought it best to hand-deliver the mail.

She arrived in a yard strewn with rusted vehicles: an ancient pickup truck, with four flat tires; hulls of dead, hulking snow machines; seized-up farm equipment, all remnants of the old farm the neighbor had inherited from his grandfather.

It was quiet except for a chainsaw moaning somewhere behind the great barn.

Near the house—a listing, 18th-century Cape Cod—the neighbor's monster truck was hiked-up on a wheel ramp. She glanced underneath: a familiar pattern struck her consciousness, like a beloved friend's face. There, on the ground, lay an antique bedspread, a linsey-woolsey coverlet, a relic fit for the wall of an old house, or a museum, even. Lying upon it: a blackened, partially disassembled starter. It was like witnessing an extinction.

At that moment, a racket seized her attention: out of the yawning barn door, two big white geese came honking and flapping her way.

She retreated promptly back down the driveway and made it out in time to place the wrongly delivered mail into the recluse's mailbox.

Flight

The orchard grass in the fretful farmer's field had grown so tall that the heads of two turkey hens—which to the lover of nature gazing out her kitchen window looked exactly like two black snakes—barely poked above the blades enough for them to keep an eye out for trouble. Invisible to the woman were the dozen or so chicks scurrying around in the weeds and grass under the two mothers, snapping up seeds and crickets and grasshoppers; but she knew they must be there, and she promptly left her kitchen perch to have a look.

She walked out her back door and strolled quietly toward the two hens, but the hens were sharp-eyed; seeing her approach, they made their way to the edge of the field where the fretful farmer's tractors had flattened a road over the years. As the woman got closer to the hens, she scanned the field but did not see any chicks. She watched as the two hens, just short of panicking, broke out of the tall grass and began to flee, virtually neck-and-neck, up the farmer's road.

Upon reaching the tallest grass, the woman paused to consider the mother hens, who now stood at the margin of the pine woods; and they, too, paused to consider her. Perhaps they were heading back to their chicks to protect them from the ape interloper. At that moment, the air in front of the woman's face exploded in a rush of feathers: a dozen or so chicks leaped up out of the grass; and before she could even fathom the hens' deception, the chicks had already sailed into the pine trees above their mothers' heads.

Pinkies

In July, the lover of nature did as the fretful farmer advised and checked her row of Red Pontiac potatoes for new tubers. As she pulled away the hay mulch, she let out a cry, as if she had received some bodily blow. There, between vines, lay a handful of *Microtus* pinkies, small as tangerine segments, hairless, wrinkled, blind. She called the fretful farmer over to ask what they were.

Not bothering to stoop for a look, staring down the full length of his standing height, the farmer declared, "Voles," in the despairing tone one would use to describe a skin ulcer.

"What should I do with them?" She stroked a pinky with her filthy forefinger. It quivered.

"Press the heel of your boot against all of them at once —"

"No!" she declared, rising out of her crouched position.

"Come here," he said, gesturing for her to follow.

Together, they walked the length of the ancient stone wall that historically divided his grandfather's property from the property of the old woman whose descendants sold out to his neighbor, the lover of nature. He pointed to a dense stand of junipers, their stems white from having been denuded of bark by hungry voles.

"This past winter they were particularly ravenous," he said.

The farmer and the lover of nature continued on into a section of the orchard replanted with new trees. In spite of the foot-high wire-wrap around the trunks, and the deer cages surrounding whole trees, voles had stripped these saplings of bark above the wire. The tops of the trees were leafless, dead.

"The snow got so deep the voles could tunnel up above the wire and chew to their hearts' content."

"But they're just babies," the neighbor lamented.

"Such sentiment is the farmer's curse," he said.

The Evening-out

The fretful farmer's new neighbor was having a hard time of it: the jet stream blew cold and dry across New England, and her apple trees had too many apples that year; so, their burdened limbs snapped in the high winds.

The worst drought in fifty years stunted the farmer's corn and killed his hay grass.

The neighbor sighed and told him, "It all evens out. There's always next year."

Indeed: the following year, the jet stream got wrapped around its own axle and trundled waves of torrential rains to the north country for months.

The storms nurtured scab fungus and bacterial blight in the woman's orchard, destroying the crop.

The farmer lamented the loss of his hay and corn to soggy ground. All his tractors became mired in mud.

He marveled at the words of his neighbor, the lover of nature: "We tend to have short memories. One year it's dry, the next wet. This will clear up."

"I guess by clear up," the fretful farmer said, "you mean clear up to your neck."

Dog Chow

As the canid loped along the country road at her mistress' side, the lover of nature marveled that she had at last found the perfect dog. She was a German Shepherd-Labrador Retriever mix, trained to be dutiful and obedient, playful and gentle with neighbors and children, a stern sentinel at home. She never bolted after small mammals while they jogged together, never strayed out of the range of her mistress's voice.

And didn't she look fetching in her reflective-orange dog parka and blue bandanna tied around her scruff!

On their run back home, the abutter's loud and obnoxious geese began to chase them down the road, and one goose got clipped by a car.

The woman took hold of her dog's collar and stepped up to the door of the house to tell the neighbor about it. Her dog sat quietly on the front porch until the neighbor got his little spaniel secured and opened the screen door to greet them.

As they spoke, the Lab immediately broke loose from her grip and bounded over the threshold— "No!"—and scampered down the hallway— "No! Come back here!"—in order to chomp down the contents of a litter box.

"I'm so sorry! That's just not like her at all!"

Bad Species

From the day the lover of nature first moved into the neighborhood, she had been immediately turned off by the neighbor whose property abutted Flyspeck Farm, for he flaunted his obnoxiousness.

He wore wraparound sunglasses and a leather cap; he had tattoos, severe lines of facial hair; he smoked; and he drove a gigantic truck with a loud muffler and a gaudy motorbike with no muffler at all.

Remarkably, every friend and associate who ever showed up in this neighbor's yard wore some variation on the themes he established or piloted a similarly hideous motor vehicle.

What horrible beliefs corresponded with their appearance, the woman did not know or care to know.

"I don't see what the attraction is," she told her neighbor, the fretful farmer. "It just makes me want to avoid them like the plague."[90]

Succession

The fretful farmer struggled to hang onto his grandfather's land, eking out hayfields, a little beef pasture, some chickens, to pay the taxes and keep him busy when he was not working.

Every so often, that is, every year or so, a little house went up on an adjacent field owned by his reclusive neighbor, looking as if it had dropped out of the sky and did not land quite squarely on its lot.

The neighbor was carving up his own grandfather's pasture lands and selling off building lots, piece by piece, to newcomers, commuters, retirees.

The farmer's other neighbor, the lover of nature, remarked: "I don't know how he can stand to look at those ugly little houses, literally in his own backyard."

"Once the carcass is carved up," the farmer said, "he'll be able to afford to move on to new pastures."

Prime

The fretful farmer's beef cattle paced along the perimeter of their exhausted pasture. October had been particularly unyielding and dry, unable to sustain all their mouths with green grass, so the farmer began giving them hay in the evenings. Only a single strand of charged, galvanized wire kept the herd out of the road and prevented them from chomping on the neighbor's flower garden.

When they arrived adjacent to the chicken house, the cows stopped and began milling around, until even the reclusive abutter noticed them. What were they so interested in at the fence line?

The abutter went over to investigate and saw they had stopped at the spot along the fence wire where the farmer had dumped a load of chicken shit and wood shavings scraped from the floor of the hen house, to be carted off later with the tractor and spread on the fields.

These cattle—the descendants of the great aurochs of the Pleistocene—were dipping their big heads close under the electric wire and extending their thick tongues towards the mixture of wood shavings and bird feces.

The abutter called the farmer over. "There's something wrong with your cows," he said.

The farmer looked over at the herd licking at the pile. "Cows look fine to me."

"But they're eating wood. You'd better feed them."

The farmer laughed. "They're not interested in the wood," he said. "I'm feeding out hay already, yet they still prefer chicken shit."

The abutter turned and began to walk away.

"They go to the butcher in a few weeks. You interested in half a side?"

Little Spaniel

The reclusive neighbor seemed not to care when his geese, as well as his little spaniel, took off after the Labrador mix coming down the road alongside her jogging partner.

While the spaniel yapped and tore after the bitch, the neighbor just flicked his cigarette over the porch rail.

The jogger managed to keep her dog under control with her voice, the larger dog staring down at the smaller one as if it were a marmot, while the geese yammered nearby.

It was clear what the little spaniel wanted from the big Lab, but the getting of it was most awkward.

"Are you going to call him off or just sit there and enjoy the show?"

"Don't worry," the neighbor said, "he's getting nowhere fast."[91]

New Owner

The fretful farmer once brought to the attention of the reclusive abutter the fact that, for years, his grandfather before him had let the farmer take the hay off the big field in exchange for upkeep of the land.

"It's mine now," the neighbor said. "I can take care of it."

The other neighbor, the lover of nature, had wondered whether it was possible for the neighbor to tell his son to drive his all-terrain vehicle more quietly on the land, and perhaps even less frequently.

"My son can do whatever he wants on my land."

His son had once asked, "Dad, why can't I sell my machine and get a bigger one?"

"Your machine? You didn't buy it."

Before she left the final time, his wife had said, "I'm sick of you trying to tell me how to live my life."

He responded, "I'll shoot any son of a bitch who trespasses on you."

Noisemakers

The din at first was shocking, stirring up in the lover of nature rage and helplessness bordering on nausea. But over time it became part of the background mayhem of the neighborhood.

Standing over her sink, scrubbing dirt from her garden turnips, digging out maggots with the point of a knife, she witnessed the windows rattling in their casings. Glancing up, she saw nothing, but she could hear it, the approaching *crescendo;* then, suddenly, on the road, large wheels and black metal zipping by, *diminuendo,* the little man—her reclusive neighbor—encased inside along with his pup, like these larvae riding inside the turnip in her hand. The noise announced to everyone that boys were on the move again.[92] They were always on the move. They never seemed to stay at home.

She paused in her washing and she breathed, focusing on these simple roots and their pest damage. She would learn to say to herself, over and over: Thank God, they keep moving. Thank God Almighty, at least they never stop.

Trapped

The fretful farmer set some steel traps to eradicate the family of marmots that were eating their way down his rows of brassicas and beans.

Every morning he came out to leafless kale stubs, gnawed broccoli heads, shorn bean stems. He placed the traps near the chucks' favorite plants and kicked a little dirt over them.

It took a couple of days of patrolling with his pistol, but one morning he came out to find a trap sprung.

It was not what he wanted to see, however: a skunk was caught there by the forelimb, a stripling.

When the farmer approached, the skunk sat up, erect and dignified, as if saying, *"Are you come at last?"*

The farmer was struck by what a handsome fellow he was. He stood far back and aimed his pistol.

The farmer shot but did not kill the skunk. It began to squirm in the trap, and the farmer shot several more times, hitting and missing the skunk.

The animal stopped moving.

The farmer reached out with a gloved hand and took hold of the chain of the trap connected to his leg.

The skunk opened its jaws and gargled, showing curved white fangs. It jerked at the trap: His feet were dark paws, clawed like a cat's.

The farmer shot it once more.[93]

The skunk went still. Then there was the remaining issue of getting the paw out of the steel trap amidst all the stench.

"Lord help you, you poor fellow," said the farmer, "why couldn't you have been the marmot?"

A Pair of Teeth

"Finally." The fretful farmer now had the pernicious marmot in his cage trap—not the flamboyant skunk, nor the feral felid, nor a pointy-faced 'possum. He threw a tarp over the cage and its terrified contents and lifted it from his rows of rodent-munched broccoli plants, their stems looking like broken matchsticks.

He would have liked to use the leg-hold trap and just shoot the critter right there amid the stems as usual, but his neighbor, the lover of nature, had pleaded with him to be humane, to "catch and release" it.

"This ain't like fishing," he had responded, only half-joking.

On his way in his truck to a secluded area a few miles away, the farmer ruminated:

When nature stumbled upon the ape, nature invented a wrench. This wrench wrenches everything towards itself.

The fallout is the same as letting nature take its course: Profligacy. Waste. Terror. And death.

Which is worse for the woodchuck: instant, violent death; or this lonesome, unrelenting terror?

Which would you choose, little marmot?

The farmer pulled off the road, took the cage out of the back of his pickup, and removed the tarp.

The marmot was bunched up inside, moist with morning dew, its fur matted with piss and shit, its teeth chattering.

This rodent was munching on nothing, nothing at all, but it was audibly munching.

Dahlia pinnata

The recluse lived on one side of Flyspeck Farm, the lover of nature on the other.

The reclusive neighbor had a boy, a pup from a previous engagement. This boy always seemed to have firecrackers on him, which randomly and spontaneously went *thump! ... thump, thump!* night and day.

The nature lover, too, was single again, a widow, and she just had her dahlias. Lots of them. They offered up brilliant, porcupine-y quills and bright, cardinally clumps to whomever cared to look.

She is kind of naïve, a hopeless romantic, concluded the fretful farmer. But in late summer her yard was awesome with the stately regalia of the dahlia, and who could fault her for that?

The boy had discovered a way to magnify the charm of his firecracker: he would sneak over to the fence where the weird lady's tall flowers were, and he would balance the firecracker perfectly across the diameter of a big, spiny bloom. Then he would light the fuse and run away.

And so, the lover of nature, like the fretful farmer, awoke to the horror of naked stems. Petals lay all over the ground like multi-colored, misshapen confetti. She was in tears over this.

Yet the farmer could not help joking about how much it looked like some marmot had mowed down her dahlias the way it mowed down his broccoli.

"Too bad you couldn't trap that little marmot and release him somewhere else," she cried.

Deer Jacking: A Romance

The lover of nature had moved to the country after her husband's death to experience something authentic, innocent, melancholy, the ache she felt upon hearing certain stringed instruments in the orchestra.

But the closer she got to nature, the uglier it seemed, a brawl of all against all. Even the plants in her garden seemed to be at each other's throats all the time.

Then she saw the reclusive neighbor's boy feeding apples to deer on the edge of her property, and she convinced herself that altruism sprouts up spontaneously from unexpected sources.

She felt buoyed up—until the night the youth returned to the forest with his father, carrying bright flashlights and rifles.

They waited for a deer to come for the apples, shot at and grazed the deer, wounding it in the eye.

The deer fled into the woods—who knew what became of it?

Then her beautiful Shepherd-Labrador mix got out one day and ran into the woods and found the animal's remains.

She rolled in the carcass then returned to the house, immensely proud of herself.

The stench was so awful it haunted the woman's dreams.

That night, her dog spoke right into her face: "Now, I can't hope to catch anything unless I can maintain my anonymity, can I?"

The Little Marmot

Like his father, the spawn of the reclusive neighbor cared nothing for the tranquility of abutters.

Like daddy, he preferred the roar of engines over the songs of bluebirds.

All day long, he sped in his all-terrain vehicle along the woods trails that snaked in and around all the adjoining properties.

Brrap! went his little engine. *Brrrap-brap!*, devouring the neighbors' peace and quiet. The boy sped back and forth, and around and around—for no reason, no reason whatsoever.

The fretful farmer's old ear had developed a dreadful callus toward all this noise, but it drove the other neighbor, the lover of nature, to near distraction.

"I don't know how I'm going to deal with it," she told the farmer.

"It helps to develop a permanent grudge against humanity," he said.

Rodent Predator

The reclusive neighbor bought his son a little air rifle that shoots BBs with a sound like *snit! snit!*

The boy went on a shooting rampage through wooded lands owned by his father, by the fretful farmer, and by the lover of nature.

All rodents were free game. It was *snit!* for *Sciurus*, *snit!* for *Tamias*, *snit! snit!* for *Marmota*. There were even *snits!* for *Erethizon*, the porcupine, the most inert of the rodents.

While walking along the road after one such shooting spree, the boy raised his air rifle and drew a bead on one of the weird lady's small sheep.

The lover of nature happened to be watching from her kitchen window, and the boy's gesture raised the hairs on the back of her head and neck.

He had no intention of shooting sheep, of course, he was just being an ass.

She quietly practiced her speech to his father over and over in her head before she delivered it to him on his porch. Loud racket and motorbikes and fireworks and dead dahlias, and now this snitting!

There was no response from the neighbor or his boy. They had no contact with her.

Even when her little sheep shed caught fire, they did not bother to come out of the house and watch the fire department hose it down.

"You can't say the crowing rooster actually caused the sun to rise," the fretful farmer told her one evening over cups of tea. "But you can bet there's a connection."

The Corn Stalkers

"Wouldn't it be nice to harvest home-grown corn-on-the-cob?" the lover of nature wondered. She set out a few long rows of seeds in her backyard and waited.

One day she glanced out her kitchen window and saw corvids trooping out of the trees and strutting around in her corn plot. They pulled every corn sprout out of the soil and ate the seed.

"What next?" she threw out, desperate.

"Replant and cover it up with a cloth," advised her neighbor, the fretful farmer. "Keep those sprouts covered until they're a foot high!"

The cloth foiled the crows; and once the tough, crinkled leaves had pushed the cloth a foot off the ground, she uncovered them to allow the stalks to straighten up and put out tassels.

Then, when the silks showed, the fretful farmer said: "If you don't spray now, you'll be eating borer larvae instead of kernels."

She bought a spray bottle of "natural" insecticide and spritzed and spritzed.

A few weeks on, the silks had turned brown and the cobs got big.

The farmer showed her how to gauge ripeness with a squeeze. "Wait another day or two," he said.

Two mornings later, she went out to find all the stalks in her corn patch flattened. Ear husks were torn open, and every cob had been chomped on.

"That sneaky raccoon!" the farmer said. "He always knows when the corn is ripe."

Horrified at the waste, the lover of nature wailed, "Why couldn't he just take his fill and leave the rest?"

"What? And leave all that nice corn for you?"

Farmer's Duty

As a youth, the fretful farmer liked to help his grandfather take care of the cows. This consisted mostly of scraping shit into a trough that transected the concrete floor of the big barn.

With a large, flat shovel he pushed piles of cow waste and soiled hay into the trough until it was full. Then he threw the switch to activate a long conveyor chain studded with scraper blades that scuttled the piles of waste out of the barn.

The waste trundled up a chute and shot out into a holding area outside the barn, where it would be dealt with later with a tractor and loader.

In January, his grandfather said, "Before chores, be sure to tap those blades and chain with the sledgehammer, then turn on the conveyor a minute to clear the ice out."

The boy only remembered this late in the morning, after he had already scraped the entire mess into the trough.

He threw the switch anyway; with a *clunk*, the chain began moving and the shit was conveyed out the barn as usual; but as the boy watched the top of the chute, he noticed that the chain was not coming back into the barn on its return run.

Instead, the whole thing catapulted out into the holding pond and disappeared in the shit.

"I forgot," was all he could say to his grandfather.

The old man went to the house and came back with a pair of hip waders. He set these down in front of the boy.

"A good whiff of cow shit does wonders for the memory."

Red Pontiacs

The fretful farmer remembers being a boy who wanted to grow crops like his grandpa before him. He chose the mighty potato (*Solanum tuberosum*), Red Pontiacs.

Grandpa provided the land and the proverbs:

"You need rich soil but stay away from sod!"

"Don't ever add lime."

"Mind the beetles!"

So, at age eleven, the incipient farmer took over a slope of the backyard, where his grandfather had ripped out some juniper bushes, and prepared his potato bed.

He dug some ancient compost out behind his grandfather's dilapidated chicken barn and worked it into the soil. He cut the seed potatoes by hand and positioned each eye into the dirt looking upward and mulched the rows over with rotted hay.

By late summer, he was digging beautiful pink jewels out of the ground. No beetles!

At age twelve, the young farmer planted a larger crop, and a few Coleopterans (*Leptinotarsa decemlineata*) showed up to the party. But he was diligent, and he picked virtually every beetle off the leaves in time to rescue the potatoes from destruction.

At age thirteen—now sporting a tiny red beard in the garden— the young farmer watched and fretted as an army of Colorado potato beetles triumphed over the Red Pontiacs.

Making Hay

While the old neighbor next door was still alive, one of the fretful farmer's hayfields was permitted to blend uninterrupted with the adjacent lot, making it a single, five-acre tract of orchard grass and tall clover. He would mow the hayfield every year, sometimes twice a year, in exchange for the upkeep of the land.

Then the old man died.

The grandson who had inherited the property never communicated his long-term intentions for the land, whether he would carve it up into house lots like the rest of the estate or not.

So, the farmer could no long count on the years-long cycles that justified the expense of liming, manuring, and maintaining the hayfield.

Meanwhile, the neighbor's boy cut a long, crooked trail-scar across the hayfield with his all-terrain vehicle.

The Fall

It was a favored pastime of the lover of nature to soak in a hot tub and look out the window into her now-denuded orchard.

Out there in the cold lay the endless pestilences and failed projects of her first attempts at farming. Inside: light, heat, and water, the order of civilization.

She appreciated the irony of being able to enjoy warm comforts behind glass while outside mayhem reigned supreme. Nothing could penetrate her bubble of contentment—until, beyond the orchard, a blazing object came into view; no, two.

They paused near a beech sapling with bronze leaves shivering.

With an awful start, she recognized the figures of her reclusive neighbor and his boy, pacing along the woods line with their guns out, their hunting outfits converging in a spectral blaze of color that hurt her eyes through the windowpanes.

Winter Bait

In February, the height of snow season, the fretful farmer saw paw prints in the snow coming out from under the barn, stepping up to the back porch, then leading away into the yard again. He put a bowl of food out on the porch and waited. He never saw the feral felid, but the food kept disappearing.

One night, he put out the food, turned on the porch light, and repeatedly looked out the window. The pointy-faced 'possum showed up on its rounds to eat out of the bowl. The fretful farmer got out his .22 pistol, but the opossum scrambled away from him, tail disappearing under the porch like a whip.

The farmer wondered to how catch a 'possum without scaring off a cat. He placed the bowl of cat food deep inside the porch, near the house entrance. Then he laid out some apple slices near a cage trap positioned at the porch door. A cat would not even glance at the apples. But an opossum would find alms.

Soon, the opossum's white, pointy face could be seen examining the inside of the cage. When the trap door slammed shut, the inside of the cage became a gray blur—and when the farmer came out with his pistol, the opossum keeled over, foaming at the mouth.

The Carnivore

The feral felid stumbled out of from under the cold barn and cast a wary eye toward the snowed-in farmhouse.

When the fretful farmer left a dish of food out for it, the carnivore accepted, and the cells in both their brains took on a sympathetic alignment.

The felid glommed onto the primate, and they became as bonded as when two apes get together, mate and have children.

Thus, this pitiless, obligate carnivore became naturalized to the world of chairs, sofas, sisal mats, bathtubs, litter boxes, catnip, and the rest.

In shows of gratitude, the felid left on the farmer's doorstep gifts of rats, mice, voles, which gifts promptly disappeared.

Signs of Spring

Winters are long on Flyspeck Farm—so much so that neighbors seem to drop out of existence. They are made known only by the sounds of their car and truck engines.

In the north country, ice-cold seems the natural state of things, as if given its druthers nature would settle this way, like water coming to rest in a low spot.

But inevitably, inconspicuously, in April, things begin happening. Peepers chirp in the snow-bound ditches.

A sciurid hops out onto the bared road surface, thinks the better of it, turns and, when the car gets too close, bunches up like a marmot in a cage trap before being crushed by tires.

And a gaudy FOR SALE sign pops up in the yard of the neighbor, the lover of nature, like a dahlia out of season.

Hawk in a Whirlwind

During the year of the drought, the fretful farmer watched from his tractor seat as his stricken corn sprouts failed in slow motion: not from his own negligence but from an intransigent jet stream that had hauled July directly into the middle of May.

The sky was a blue void that would not admit rain.

The farmer could not replant in this dry ground, so the fields became populated with plants that bore animals' names: crabgrass, goosefoot, pigweed, cow parsnip, chickweed, oxeye daisy, coltsfoot, rattlesnake weed, horsenettle, toadflax. These thrive in hot, malignant weather.

Driving back to the barn, the farmer's tractor tires kicked up a dust storm. A vortex lifted the dust of the field and some of last year's leaves into a cylinder that twisted over his head. Glancing up, he saw a *Buteo jamaicensis* sail headlong into the top of this whirlwind.

Turning and backing off, the hawk flapped in the opposite direction, shrieking and soaring, as if suddenly elated by the knowledge that he has nothing to his name.

Acknowledgments

"Pinkies" was first published in *Unlimited Literature* (UL-Mag), July 2020.

The parable "The Worm" appeared in *Tiny Seed Literary Journal Flash Fiction Project*, February 2020.

The parable "Dog-Eat-Ape World" is included in the anthology *Neighbors* published by Crack the Spine Press in 2020.

"Rhinoceros, Run," was published in *Meat for Tea: The Valley Review*, Vol. 13, Issue 2, 2019.

"Pigs at the Trough" appeared as "Gluttony: A Parable," in *Meat for Tea: The Valley Review*, Vol. 13, Issue 1, 2019.

The parable "Fertility" won Two Sisters Writing & Publishing Flash Fiction Award, February 2019.

"The Porcupine Tree," "Deer Jacking: A Romance," and "The Corn Stalkers" were published as "Three Parables from Flyspeck Farm," in *The Ilanot Review*, summer 2018.

"Tribes," "Monitor Lizard *contra* Cobra," "To Be a Bat," "Preening," "A Pastoral Parable," appeared as "Cautionary Fables for Darwin's Birthday," at *3QuarksDaily*, 3quarksdaily.com, February 12, 2018.

"The Smiling Toads of Darwin's Bluff," "The Flounder's Eye," and "From Froglet to True Frog" first appeared as "Three Fables to Commemorate Darwin's Birthday," at *3QuarksDaily*, 3quarksdaily.com, February 13, 2017.

"Ants vs. Termites," "Tetrapods," "Ruminants," and "Parrots," were published in *3QuarksDaily*, 3quarksdaily.com, October 10, 2016.

Thanks are due to the following: S. Abbas Raza, for taking an early interest in these fables at the website *3 Quarks Daily*; Professor Kenneth Weber, Biology, and Professor Marcia Anne-Dobres, Anthropology, whose courses at the University of Southern Maine inspired several of these tales; Michele Cheung, also of USM, who gave me a reading platform for these works at Southworth Planetarium over the years of their composition; Claudia and Ken, whose Maine farm is both home and model for Flyspeck Farm; Mom and Dad, who advised me to never give up; and my husband, Don, for decades of patience and support.

Photo courtesy of Donna Katsiaficas

Mike Bendzela was born in Ohio and received his BA from the University of Toledo. After earning an MA at SUNY-Binghamton in 1985, he moved to a farm in Maine, where he has been ever since. Early on, he published in national literary magazines and anthologies, receiving a Pushcart Prize in 1992. He took a long hiatus from writing to learn Old Time fiddle and banjo, work as an on-call EMT, and start a small market farm and heritage orchard. He began submitting work again in 2017, publishing a novella and receiving an award for flash fiction. *Metazoan Variations* is a four-year project that combines his life-long interest in evolutionary biology with the narrative arts. He teaches at the University of Southern Maine and lives with his husband on the farm, which they share with an assortment of felids and other animals.

Notes

[1] I do not include the roughly 38% who "believe" that humans developed over time "with God guiding." That is not the naturalism that Darwin espoused, that's supernaturalism, just another form of creationism. "In U.S., Belief in Creationist View of Humans at New Low." Gallup Poll, May 22, 2017. https://news.gallup.com/poll/210956/belief-creationist-view-humans-new-low.aspx.

[2] Goldsmith, Oliver. *Treasury of Aesop's Fable* (New York: Avenel Books, 1973), *iii.*

[3] Ibid.

[4] Goldsmith, p. 103.

[5] Young, David. *The Discovery of Evolution.* (UK: Cambridge University Press, 2007), p. 16.

[6] Ibid.

[7] Darwin, Charles. *The Descent of Man and Selection in Relation to Sex.* (New York: Penguin Books, 2004).

[8] "Origin of man now proved.—Metaphysic must flourish.—He who understands baboon would do more towards metaphysics than Locke."—Charles Darwin, 1838: *Notebook M.*

[9] "'This is [...] a classic case of convergent evolution: both groups evolved similar molecular mechanisms for a eusocial lifestyle under similar selection pressures,' says genomics expert Dr. Mark Harrison." "The social evolution of termites: Similar genes involved in the evolution of insect societies as in bees and ants." *ScienceDaily.* www.sciencedaily.com/releases/2018/02/180207142716.htm

[10] "All that we can do, is to keep steadily in mind that each organic being is striving to increase in a geometric ratio; that each at some period of its life, during some season of the year, during each generation or at intervals, has to struggle for life and to suffer great destruction." Charles Darwin, *On the Origin of Species,* (New York: The Modern Library, 1996) p. 106.

[11] "I cannot persuade myself that a beneficent & omnipotent God would have designedly created the Ichneumonidae with the express intention of their feeding within the living bodies of caterpillars...." Charles Darwin, to Asa Gray, 22 May 1860. *Darwin Correspondence Project.* University of Cambridge, 2016. http://www.darwinproject.ac.uk/

[12] "I believe that many lowly organized forms now exist throughout the world, from various causes. [...] [T]he main cause lies in the fact that under very simple conditions of life a high organisation would be of no service. [...]" *Origin of Species*, p. 164.

[13] Darwin's euphonious, pre-Mendelian term attempting to posit a particle-

217

based inheritance principle.

[14] "…ticks have become so voracious in some places a single moose can carry an appalling 90,000 at once …. In such numbers the ticks drain so much blood that the host moose can become anemic and malnourished…." Laura Poppick, "As Winters Warm, Blood-sucking Ticks Drain Moose Dry." *Scientific American,* December 11, 2018.

[15] A stunning *National Geographic* video of this phenomenon may be found here: https://video.nationalgeographic.com/video/untamed/00000162-300f-ddf6-a5eb-712f562a0000

[16] A good account of this unusual critter is available at Jerry Coyne's website *Why Evolution Is True* under the title "You won't believe how this crazy spider tricks females into mating."

[17] Pareidolia: "A type of illusion or misperception involving a vague or obscure stimulus being perceived as something clear and distinct." Robert Todd Carroll, *Becoming a Critical Thinker: A Guide for the New Millennium* (Boston, MA: Pearson Custom Publishing, 2005) p. 238.

[18] "Walking sticks are a favorite food of many animals, but perhaps their most effective predators are bats. Most bats hunt by echolocation rather than sight, so they aren't fooled by the insect's sticklike appearance." "Walking Sticks." The National Wildlife Federation. https://www.nwf.org/Educational-Resources/Wildlife-Guide/Invertebrates/Walking-Sticks

[19] According to Dr. Sam Gon's "A Guide to the Orders of Trilobites," there are over "20,000 described species" of trilobites. "New species of trilobites are unearthed and described every year. This makes trilobites the single most diverse class of extinct organisms, and within the generalized body plan of trilobites there was a great deal of diversity of size and form." http://www.trilobites.info/index.htm

[20] "*Ophiocordyceps unilateralis* […] is a specialized parasite that infects, manipulates and kills formicine ants, predominantly in tropical forest ecosystems. […] On [the] infected carpenter ant […] the fungus [is] characterized macroscopically by a single stalk arising from the dorsal neck region on which the sexual structures [. . .] are borne laterally. […]" Evans, H. C., Elliot, S. L., & Hughes, D. P. (2011). "Ophiocordyceps unilateralis: A keystone species for unraveling ecosystem functioning and biodiversity of fungi in tropical forests?" *Communicative & integrative biology*, 4(5), pp. 598-602.

[21] At Jerry Coyne's website, *Why Evolution Is True*, there are photographs of these two arthropods and a link to the article by Mather, M. H., and B. D. Roitberg, 1987, "A sheep in wolf's clothing: Tephritid flies mimic spider predators." Science 236:308-10.

[22] "[E]volutionary change, even of a major sort, nearly always involves remodeling the old into the new. [. . .] whales are stretched-out land animals

whose forelimbs have become paddles and whose nostrils have moved atop their heads." Jerry A. Coyne. *Why Evolution Is True* (New York: Penguin Group, 2009) p. 53.

[23] The odd paradox of a brain that seems expressly designed not to grasp evolution was noted by Darwin: "[T]he chief cause of our unwillingness to admit that one species has given birth to clear and distinct species, is that we are always slow in admitting great changes of which we do not see the steps. . . . The mind cannot possibly grasp the full meaning of the term of even a million years; it cannot add up and perceive the full effects of many slight variations, accumulated during an almost infinite number of generations. [...] I by no means expect to convince experienced naturalists whose minds are stocked with a multitude of facts all viewed, during a long course of years, from a point of view directly opposite to mine." *Origin of Species,* p. 639.

[24] "*D. pedunculatus* usually [. . .] carries sea anemones on its shell, which it uses to protect itself from its main predator, cephalopods of the genus *Octopus*. The anemones are collected at night, and comprises the crab stroking and tapping the anemone until it loosens its grip on the substrate, at which point it is moved onto the gastropod shell that the hermit crab inhabits." Wikipedia, *Dardanus pedunculatus.*

[25] "[T]he earliest creature to have the bones of our upper arm, our forearm, even our wrist and palm, also had scales and fin webbing. That creature was a fish." Neil Shubin, *Your Inner Fish* (New York: Random House, 2009) p. 41. Also: "...we may ... venture to believe that the several bones in the limbs of the monkey, horse, and bat, were originally developed, on the principle of utility, probably through the reduction of more numerous bones in the fin of some ancient fish-like progenitor of the whole class." Darwin, *Origin of Species,* p. 252

[26] In a letter to J. D. Hooker, 1 Feb 1871, Darwin speculates about "some warm little pond" where life may have begun. Darwin Correspondence Project: University of Cambridge. www.darwinproject.ac.uk/letter/DCP-LETT-7471.xml

[27] "[A child] is too small and weak to bully its parents physically, but it uses every psychological weapon at its disposal: lying, cheating, deceiving, exploiting. [...]" Richard Dawkins, *The Selfish Gene.* (Oxford, UK: Oxford University Press, 1989), p. 131.

[28] Field studies have shown that bowerbirds employ "forced perspective" resembling that of painters to "make courts with gray and white objects that increase in size with distance from the avenue entrance." From the female viewer's perspective, this creates a "false perception of size and distance." Endler, J. et al. "Great Bowerbirds Create Theaters with Forced Perspective When Seen by Their Audience." *Current Biology*. Volume 20, Issue 18, pp.

1679–1684.

[29] Some brood parasites such as *Molothrus* exhibit "mafia-like retaliatory behavior" on "ejector nests," meaning that if the host bird rejects the parasitic bird's eggs or young, the parasite will return to the nest and destroy it and the host's young. Jeffrey P. Hoover, Scott K. Robinson, "Retaliatory mafia behavior by a parasitic cowbird favors host acceptance of parasitic eggs," *Proceedings of the National Academy of Science*, March 13, 2007; 104 (11), 4483.

[30] "Following the sudden demise of the dinosaurs, the snake *Titanoboa* was the largest land hunter of the Paleocene. [...] [Its] enormous vertebrae were found in coal deposits in Colombia, along with the remains of the crocodiles and turtles [it] preyed upon." *Prehistoric life: The definitive history of life on Earth* (New York: DK Publishing, 2012), p. 377.

[31] Darwin rebuts the argument that "as none of the animals and plants of Egypt [. . .] have changed during the last three or four thousand years, so probably have none in any part of the world," with the observation that this period of time is as nothing compared to that which has elapsed "since the commencement of the glacial period." The "ancient domestic races" he refers to, which so resemble those in existence today, have not changed because in places like Egypt, "during the last several thousand years, the conditions of life, as far as we know have remained absolutely uniform." *Origin of Species,* pp. 264-265.

[32] "Just as genes propagate themselves in the gene pool by leaping from body to body via sperm or eggs, so memes propagate themselves in the meme pool by leaping from brain to brain via a process which, in the broad sense, can be called imitation." Richard Dawkins, *The Selfish Gene,* p. 192.

[33] This is Batesian mimicry. "Bates [...] observed that the imitating species are comparatively rare, whilst the imitated abound, and that the two sets live mingled together. [...] [H]e concluded that [the imitated species] must be protected from the attacks of enemies by some secretion or odour; and this conclusion has now been amply confirmed. [...] Mr Bates inferred that the [species] which imitate the protected species have acquired their present marvellously deceptive appearance through variation and natural selection, in order to be mistaken for the protected kinds, and thus to escape being devoured." Charles Darwin, *The Descent of Man,* p. 369.

[34] This phenomenon is called the Red Queen hypothesis, a term coined by Leigh Van Halen. It weds a Darwinian idea to the character from Lewis Carroll's *Through the Looking Glass* who claims that one must run harder just to stand still. "In the world of the Red Queen, any evolutionary progress will be relative as long as your foe is animate and depends heavily on you or suffers heavily if you thrive. [...] Thus the Red Queen will be especially hard at work among predators and their prey." Matt Ridley, *The Red Queen.* (New York:

Penguin 1993), p. 19.

[35] No one knows whether Archaeopteryx actually took wing. Darwin's "wondrous Bird," "the greatest fossil of our times," is best known for its excitement of the imagination. (Darwin quotes come from Gene Kritky, "Darwin's Archaeopteryx *prophecy*," *Archives of Natural History* 19 (3): 407-410. http://faculty.msj.edu/kritskg/darwin/Site/Darwin_Miscellany_files/Archaeopteryx.pdf)

[36] Richard Goldschmidt is quoted by Ernst Mayr as saying, "...the first bird hatched from a reptilian egg" (which is true only insofar as Aves are included in the Reptilian class). *Ornithology, Evolution, and Philosophy.* (Heidelberg, Germany: Springer-Verlag, 2008) p. 196. Such sentiments were common among the mutationists, who (in violation of Leibnitz's principle *Natura non facit saltum*) were simply incredulous that new species could arrive on scene through the incremental processes of natural selection.

[37] "As many as 30 percent of Canada geese, one of the most ubiquitous birds in North America, may in fact be so disposed—something we'd probably notice more if the sexes didn't look so much alike that only people who make a habit of studying them can tell the difference." Keim, Brandon. "Why Are So Many Animals Homosexual?" *Nautilus.* February 23, 2016. http://nautil.us/blog/why-are-so-many-animals-homosexual

[38] "Perhaps the most remarkable instance of an immense bird population is that of the passenger pigeon of the United States, which lays only one, or at most two eggs, and is said to rear generally but one young one. Why is this bird so extraordinarily abundant, while others producing two or three times as many young are much less plentiful? ...The food most congenial to this species, and on which it thrives best, is abundantly distributed over a very extensive region, offering such differences of soil and climate, that in one part or another of the area the supply never fails. [...] This example strikingly shows us that the procuring a constant supply of wholesome food is almost the sole condition requisite for ensuring the rapid increase of a given species." Alfred Russel Wallace, *On the Tendency of Varieties to depart indefinitely from the Original Type.* Darwin Online website. http://darwin-online.org.uk/content/frameset?itemID=F350&viewtype=text&pageseq=1

[39] "[Natural] selection is not a mechanism imposed on a population from outside. Rather, it is a *process*, a description of how genes that produce better adaptations become more frequent over time. When biologists say selection is acting 'on' a trait, they're merely using shorthand to say that the trait is undergoing the process. In the same sense, species don't try to adapt to their environment. There is no will involved, no conscious striving. Adaptation to the environment is inevitable if a species has the right kind of genetic

variation." Coyne, *Why Evolution Is True,* p. 117.

[40] "In a long-term study, Canestrari *et al.* found that crow nests containing a cuckoo chick had lower rates of predation because the parasite's chicks secrete a noxious repellent substance." "From Parasitism to Mutualism: Unexpected Interactions between a Cuckoo and Its Host." *Science* 21 Mar 2014: Vol. 343, Issue 6177, pp. 1350-1352.

[41] The turkey hen commits the same "Type 1" error as *Equus* in "The Late *Dinohippus,*" the false positive. This assume-the-worst, "better safe than sorry" mental heuristic may account for much discrimination.

[42] Among these were our ancestors, the early Eutherians, such as *Eomaia,* whose "name means 'dawn mother,' reflecting its crucial position within our own family tree. [...] Tall, sharp points, or cusps, on its teeth suggest that it was a predator of insects and other small mammals." *Prehistoric life: The definitive history of life on Earth,* p. 357.

[43] *Dinohippus,* once the most common horse in North America up until the Pliocene Epoch, was probably the precursor to the modern *Equus.* That *Dinohippus* went extinct due to its lack of caution is, of course, pure fancy.

[44] *Equus* is making a "*Type I error* of cognition, also known as a *false positive,* or believing something is real when it is not." Michael Shermer calls this a "non-existent pattern. [...] No harm. You move away from the rustling sound, become more alert and cautious, and find another path to your destination." *The Believing Brain* (New York: Times Books, 2011) p. 59.

[45] *Dinohippus* has succumbed to a *Type II error,* the *false negative,* "believing something is not real when it is. That is, you have missed a real pattern. You failed to connect (A) a rustle in the grass to (B) a dangerous predator, and in this case A was connected to B. You're lunch" (Ibid). One can make as many *Type I* errors as one wishes without harm, but one need only make a single *Type II* error to be selected out of the gene pool. Hence, our natural tendency toward what Shermer calls "patternicity" and a heightened sense of suspicion.

[46] Wadi Al-Hitan, the whale valley, site of Eocene seabed and whale fossils.

[47] In a lecture, "Free Will is as Real as Colors, Promises and Euros," Daniel Dennett describes "Gibsonian affordances," or opportunities in the environment that species are adapted to. He notes that "birds that are insectivores [...] track individual insects [...] whereas the anteater doesn't track individual ants, any more than we track individual sugar molecules or water molecules. [...] it's just stuff. So the anteater sticks out its sticky tongue and *slurp!* gets a whole lotta ant." It scarcely makes a difference, then, that the affordances here are termites.
https://www.youtube.com/watch?reload=9&v=G8DQfYV49gI

[48] Darwin reflects on species that share "much similarity in habits and constitution," noting that the struggle amongst them "will generally be more severe [...] if they come into competition with each other. [...] We can dimly

see why the competition should be most severe between allied forms, which fill nearly the same place in nature; but probably in no one case could we precisely say why one species has been victorious over another in the great battle of life." *Origin of Species,* pp. 104-106.

[49] "There is no exception to the rule that every organic being naturally increases at so high a rate, that, if not destroyed, the earth would soon be covered by the progeny of a single pair." *Origin of Species,* p. 91.

[50] Like the panda's thumb Stephen Jay Gould discusses, the sciurid's flaps are "a somewhat clumsy, but quite workable, solution" to the issue of flight from predators. "Odd arrangements and funny solutions are the proof of evolution." *The Panda's Thumb: More Reflections in Natural History.* (New York: W. W. Norton & Company, 1980), pp. 19-26.

[51] Apophenia: "Perceiving patterns where there are none." Carroll, *Becoming a Critical Thinker,* p. 235.

[52] This is based on the *Wikipedia* entry on the North American beaver, which contains language that veers close to expressing a "promiscuous teleology" (a term coined by Deborah Kelemen of Boston University), with the beneficent beaver as the stand-in for Yahweh, the Intelligent Designer.

[53] "Star-nosed moles can identify and eat a small prey item in as little as 120 msec, with an average time of 230 msec. This finding literally placed them in the Guinness Book of World Records as the fastest foragers among mammals." Catania, Kenneth C. "A Nose for Touch." *The Scientist.* September 1, 2012.

[54] There is no "playing 'possum" with the phenomenon of apparent death, "an involuntary physiological response similar to fainting that causes the opossum to appear and smell like a dead or dying animal, thereby deterring predators who generally prefer live prey. An opossum will remain unconscious anywhere from thirty minutes to four hours." *Discover Magazine.* http://discovermagazine.com/sitefiles/resources/image.aspx?item=%7B3BCD D253-B27B-4B1D-AA6B-86216EA04880%7D

[55] "Male chimpanzees at the Gombe National Park were twice seen to attack 'stranger' females and seize their infants. One infant was then killed and partially eaten." Goodall, J. "Infant killing and cannibalism in free-living chimpanzees." *Folia Primatol* 28(4):259-89. This fable is based on memories inspired by this horrific video: http://www.dailymotion.com/video/x2qd2zk

[56] "The habitual use of articulate language is [...] peculiar to man; but he uses, in common with the lower animals, inarticulate cries to express his meaning. [...] This especially holds good with the more simple and vivid feelings.... Our cries of pain, fear, surprise, anger, together with the appropriate actions [...] are more expressive than any words." Darwin, *The Descent of Man,* p. 107.

[57] "The use of 'tactical deception' is argued to have been important in the cognitive evolution of the order Primates. [...] [A]larm calls are used by

capuchins to reduce the effects of feeding competition. Whether this is intentional on the part of the caller requires further investigation." Brandon C. Wheeler, "Monkeys crying wolf?" http://rspb.royalsocietypublishing.org/content/276/1669/3013.

[58] "A highly successful and widespread genus of mammoths, *Mammuthus* lived across the northern continents and Africa throughout the Pliocene and Pleistocene epochs. [...] [M]ammoths were hunted by humans all over the world and that, along with the effects of climate changes, probably contributed to their extinction." *Prehistoric life*, p. 437.

[59] Some of the earliest cave paintings are interpreted as female vulvae, from as long as 37,000 years ago. https://www.the-scientist.com/the-nutshell/vulva-cave-art-41001

[60] "*Coelodonta*, the woolly rhinoceros, lived in ice-age North America and Eurasia. It became extinct 10,000 years ago—after humans arrived." *Prehistoric life*, p. 33.

[61] This figure is inspired, roughly, by The Sorcerer of *Grotte des Trois Frères*.

[62] Adapted from Chapter 7, "Hunting," *The Old Way*, Elizabeth Marshall Thomas (New York: Farrar, Straus and Giroux, 2006).

[63] Whether or not farming is "The Worst Mistake in the History of the Human Race," as Jared Diamond says, it was clearly a sort of phase change in human development, and we're unlikely to go back to the way it was before. Like the emergence of species, the old must give way to the new, although the new will at first be vigorously resisted.

[64] Cultural innovations behave like new species: "...each new variety or species, during the progress of its formation, will generally press hardest on its nearest kindred, and tend to exterminate them." Darwin, *Origin of Species,* p. 142.

[65] "Although spirochetes are not a large group—there are only six genera—they have had tremendous impact on our lives. Both syphilis and Lyme disease are caused by these bacteria, and other species are important symbionts in the stomachs of cows and other ruminants." *Introduction to the Spirochetes.* http://www.ucmp.berkeley.edu/bacteria/spirochetes.html

[66] In their long-term study of olive baboons in Kenya, Robert Sapolsky and Lisa Share encountered this phenomenon when alpha males became infected with bovine tuberculosis in a trash dump. "Emergence of a Peaceful Culture in Wild Baboons." https://doi.org/10.1371/journal.pbio.0020124.

[67] "Sapolsky and Share are still unsure how the culture is being passed on, but they suspect that it has to do with the observed friendly attitude of the female baboons towards newcomer males." Kim Krieger, "A Kinder, Gentler Baboon." *Science.* April 13, 2004.

[68] A made-up organism, but mimicking effects proposed to occur in humans by latent infection of *Toxoplasma gondii.*

[69] "No one would have thought of teaching, or probably could have taught, the tumbler-pigeon to tumble, an action which [...] is performed by young birds, that have never seen a pigeon tumble. [...] [Near] Glasgow there are house-tumblers [...] which cannot fly eighteen inches without going head over heels." *Origin of Species,* p. 325.

[70] De Waal's and Bronan's famous fairness experiment, with the dry line, "Negative reactions may occur when expectations are violated." "Monkeys reject unequal pay." *Nature* 425, (18 September 2003) pp. 297-299.

[71] Both Darwin and Wallace expressed something of the despair and dismay of studying this feature of nature so intently: "I have found it hard constantly to bear in mind that the increase of every single species is checked during some part of its life, or during some shortly recurrent generation. Only a few of those annually born can live to propagate their kind. What a trifling difference must often determine which shall survive, and which perish!" (*Abstract of a Letter from* C. Darwin, Esq., *to* Prof. Asa Gray, *Boston, U.S., dated Down, September 5th,* 1857.) "With such powers of increase the population must have reached its limits. [...] It is evident, therefore, that each year an immense number [...] must perish—as many in fact as are born; and as on the lowest calculation the progeny are each year twice as numerous as their parents, it follows that, whatever be the average number of individuals existing in any given country, *twice that number must perish annually,*—a striking result, but one which seems at least highly probable, and is perhaps under rather than over the truth." Alfred Russel Wallace, *Infinite Tropics: An Alfred Russel Wallace Anthology,* edited by Andrew Berry (New York: Verso, 2002).

[72] In a chapter about "one of the classic transitions in all of evolution," Donald Prothero reminds us that the term "amphibian" is "antiquated" and that "most modern cladistic classifications schemes [...] use the natural monophyletic group known as tetrapods" to describe our fishy ancestors and their descendants. *Evolution: What the Fossils Say and Why It Matters.* (New York: Columbia University Press, 2007) p. 217.

[73] "History of error" is Charles Darwin's dismissive phrase for previous hypotheses, such as his grandfather Erasmus Darwin's belief in Lamarckian transmutation theory. ("To T. H. Huxley 9 January [1860]"). Darwin Correspondence Project. https://www.darwinproject.ac.uk/letter/DCP-LETT-2646.xml

[74] Discovered in 2004, this "new creature broke down the distinction between" land-living animals and fish. "Like a fish, it has scales on its back and fins with fin webbing. But, like early land-living animals, it has a flat head and a neck." Neil Shubin, *Your Inner Fish* (New York: Vintage Books, 2009), p. 23.

[75] "[A] classic fishibian: limbs and spine like a tetrapod, but tail fin, and lateral line canals like a fish." Prothero, *Evolution,* p. 229).

[76] One of the first amniote tetrapods to lay eggs on dry land, *Anthracosaurus*

had specialized bones in its neck that allowed them "to swivel their heads and rapidly to catch prey." Prothero, *Evolution,* p. 235).

[77] A fictional organism named after the Proterozoic Era; the elusive first metazoan.

[78] "The season of love is that of battle; but the males of some birds [...] are ready to fight whenever they meet. The presence of the female is the *teterrima belli causa* ['most shameful cause of war'—Horace]." Darwin, *The Descent of Man*, p. 415.

[79] "It is almost superfluous to state that animals have excellent *Memories* for persons and places. [...] Animals can certainly by some means judge of the intervals of time between recurrent events." Darwin, *Descent of Man*, p. 95.

[80] Surplus killing is a well-known phenomenon. Marc Baldwin has a good discussion on wildlifeonline.me.uk, which summarizes the findings of Hans Kruuk, Professor of Zoology at Aberdeen University: "Indeed [...] hunting depends on both prey and environment, coupled with the predator's own motivation and hunger. *If prey is easily available (i.e. none of the risks associated with the chase and capture are present), then a predator doesn't need to be hungry to readily take the quarry. This scenario—where a predator kills without the motivation of hunger, or kills more than is necessary to sate its hunger—is referred to as Surplus Killing.*" The stoat's rationalization of its instinct is, of course, fanciful.

[81] "The mind is primed to react emotionally to the sight of snakes, not just to fear them but to be aroused and absorbed in their details, to weave stories about them. [...] The rule built into the brain in the form of a learning bias is: become alert quickly to any object with the serpentine gestalt. *Overlearn* this particular response in order to keep safe. Other primates have evolved similar rules." Edward O. Wilson, *Biophilia* (Cambridge, Massachusetts: Harvard University Press, 1984), pp. 86, 93.

[82] "The essential difference in the conditions of wild and domestic animals is this—that among the former, their well-being and very existence depend upon the full exercise and healthy condition of all their senses and physical powers, whereas, among the latter, these are only partially exercised, and in some cases are absolutely unused....Half of its senses and faculties are quite useless; and the other half are but occasionally called into feeble exercise, while even its muscular system is only irregularly called into action." Alfred Russel Wallace, *Infinite Tropics*, p. 59.

[83] This observation around the farm has been confirmed by research done by Dr. Charles E. Roselli, Oregon Health & Science University School of Medicine. "My laboratory discovered a sex difference in part of the sheep brain [...] that's known to control sexual behaviors. The difference consists of the size of a cluster of neurons in the preoptic area, which we named the ovine sexually dimorphic nucleus or oSDN. [...] Approximately 8% of adult rams

prefer to mount other rams instead of ewes." ohsu.edu.

[84] "Horses are very one-sided because they have a very underdeveloped corpus callosum, which is the connective tissue between the two hemispheres of the brain. [...] that's why you train a horse on one side and then you have to go back and train them completely on the other side." Julie Goodnight, "Left Brain, Right Brain." *America's Horse Daily,* 29 Sep 15.

[85] Wallace notes in his Ternate paper that animals with domestically selected traits are not adapted to the wild. "Even a change of color might, by rendering them more or less distinguishable, affect their safety." As Darwin says, the traits of wild species are continually being tested; "natural selection is daily and hourly scrutinizing, throughout the world, every variation,"; whereas a domestic animal—which in Wallace's words is "abnormal, irregular, artificial"—is continually being provided for by its human captor, so its traits escape natural selection. In consequence, "Domestic varieties, when turned wild, *must* return to something near the type of the original wild stock, *or become altogether extinct." Infinite Tropics,* p. 57.

[86] "It requires a deliberate mental effort to turn biology the right side up [...] and remind ourselves that the replicators come first, in importance as well as in history." Dawkins, *The Selfish Gene,* p. 265.

[87] Equine Protozoal Myeloencephalitis. "[T]he organism Sarcocystis neurona is spread by the definitive host, the opossum.... The infective stage of the organism (the sporocysts) is passed in the opossum's feces. The horse comes into contact with the infective sporocysts while grazing or eating contaminated feed or drinking water." https://aaep.org/horsehealth/epm-understanding-debilitating-disease

[88] Another instance of "surplus killing." See "The Stoat's Reasoning."

[89] "A unique kind of antipredator defense is the shedding of parts of the body (autotomy) as a means of escape. [...] The tail is generally lost because that is the part of the body that is closest to the predator." Anders Pape Møller, Jan Tøttrup Nielsen, Johannes Erritzøe, "Losing the last feather: feather loss as an antipredator adaptation in birds," *Behavioral Ecology,* Volume 17, Issue 6, pp. 1046–1056. https://doi.org/10.1093/beheco/arl044

[90] As in Mullerian mimicry, "the general phenomenon of evolved similarity among unpalatable species," these individuals have converged on a design that advertises their "unprofitability." Sherratt, Thomas N. "The evolution of Mullerian mimicry." Naturwissenschaften. 2008 Aug; 95(8): pp. 681–695.

[91] "[T]he domestic varieties of the same species differ from each other in almost every character, which man has attended to and selected, more than do the distinct species of the same genera." Darwin, *Origin of Species,* p. 63.

[92] "Recent studies have revealed that some mammals possess adaptations that enable them to produce vocal signals with much lower fundamental frequency

and formant frequency spacing than expected for their size." "The evolution of acoustic size exaggeration in terrestrial mammals." Benjamin D. Charlton & David Reby. *Nature Communications* volume 7, Article number: 12739 (2016).

[93] In his Autobiography, Darwin expresses regret for his youthful "zeal" for killing animals. As he got older, "I gave up my gun more and more. […] I discovered, though unconsciously and insensibly, that the pleasure of observing and reasoning was a much higher one than that of skill and sport. The primeval instincts of the barbarian slowly yielded to the acquired tastes of the civilized man." His studies gradually matured him into a being who rued the "sufferings of millions of the lower animals throughout almost endless time." *The Autobiography of Charles Darwin.* Online. https://www.gutenberg.org/files/2010/2010-h/2010-h.htm